THE EARTH, MY B
AND OTHER BiG, ROUND THINGS

When Carolyn Mackler was seventeen, she left her homeland of western New York to attend Vassar College, study in Paris, drive across the United States in a car named Egg and live in eleven different apartments, two half-of-houses and one tent. She eventually made her way to New York City and became a writer. The author of the best-selling books for young adults *Love and Other Four-Letter Words* and *Vegan, Virgin, Valentine*, she was awarded a prestigious Printz Honor in the USA for *The Earth, My Butt and Other Big, Round Things*. Carolyn has appeared on television, on radio programmes and in schools, where her favourite question so far has been "Do any of your main characters have freckles?" She is recently married, and lives in New York City with her husband.

Also by Carolyn Mackler

Love and Other Four-Letter Words
Vegan, Virgin, Valentine

THE EARTH MY BUTT and other BiG round THiNGS

carolyn mackler

WALKER BOOKS
AND SUBSIDIARIES
LONDON · BOSTON · SYDNEY · AUCKLAND

Acknowledgments

Thanks to my agent, Jodi Reamer, whose positive attitude
drove this novel forward. Thanks to my U.S. and U.K.
editors, Deborah Wayshak and Mara Bergman, for loving
Virginia as much as I do. Thanks to Liz Bicknell, Jane
Winterbotham, and all the amazing people at Candlewick
and Walker. Thanks to everyone who gave me the scoop on
private schools, plus sizes, piercing, and so much more.
Thanks to Jenny Greenberg, Amber Kallen-Monroe, and
Juliet Siler, for reading the manuscript and offering valuable
suggestions. And a special thanks to my family and friends,
for always making me feel welcome on this earth.

First published 2003 by Walker Books Ltd
87 Vauxhall Walk, London SE11 5HJ

8 10 9 7

Text © 2003 Carolyn Mackler
Cover design by Walker Books Ltd

The right of Carolyn Mackler to be identified as author
of this work has been asserted by her in accordance with the
Copyright, Designs and Patents Act 1988

This book has been typeset in Sabon, Matisse,
Providence-Dingbats, Vladimir Script, FF Hands,
Kosmik-Glyphs, Helvetica Neue Condensed
and Tekton MM

Printed in Great Britain by Cox & Wyman Ltd, Reading, Berkshire

British Library Cataloguing in Publication Data:
a catalogue record for this book is
available from the British Library

ISBN 0-7445-9077-9

www.walkerbooks.co.uk

To Jonas Rideout,
for listening and laughing and loving

CHAPTER ONE

Froggy Welsh the Fourth is trying to get up my shirt.

This is the third Monday that he's come over to my apartment after school. Every week we go a little further, and today, on September twenty-third at 3:17 P.M., he's begun inching his fingers across my stomach and toward my bra.

"Virginia?"

I'm not sure whether Froggy is saying my name as a prelude to a question or whether he's uttering it in ecstasy. As much as I wish it were the latter, I conclude that it's the former. We're only fifteen, after all.

"Yeah?" I ask.

"Is it OK if I...?" Froggy rubs his nose a few times. He's always tweaking his nose. I think it's an anxiety thing. "Would you mind if I...?"

7

"I … errr," I say. "I mean … ummm … yeah."

Not exactly the sensuous dialogue you conjure up when you imagine your first time reaching second base. But Froggy and I don't score high on the communication front. Especially once we've stuck our tongues into each other's mouths.

I think it's because we're not boyfriend and girl-friend, or even *friends*, for that matter. Until the beginning of tenth grade, Froggy and I just pass-ed each other in the halls at school, sometimes waving, sometimes saying hi, sometimes doing nothing at all. Which is pretty much how it still is, except for this kissing aspect. I can't say it's what I want, but I know this is all it can ever be.

It's not like Froggy Welsh the Fourth is a huge catch. First of all, there's his name. Not a nickname for Frank or Frederick or even *Frog*. I'm still shock-ed that his great-great-grandparents named a son Froggy. But what astounds me to no end is that three subsequent generations decided to follow suit.

Froggy is medium height and slender. His ruf-fled blond hair crests into a cowlick. His dollop of a nose reminds me of a lamb's snout. Especially since it's always pinkish, probably from so much tweaking. Whenever his pubescent voice cracks, he sounds like a screeching chicken. Put his name and traits together and you've got a farm.

But he's here.

And he's a halfway decent kisser.

 8

Maybe it's all the trombone lessons.

Trombone is the reason we've been fooling around since the beginning of the school year. Froggy takes Monday-afternoon trombone lessons from a student at Juilliard. That's this prestigious music school on the West Side of Manhattan, about fifteen blocks from my apartment. Brewster, our small private school, is on the East Side. Every Monday we ride the crosstown bus together.

On the first Monday of the school year, Froggy slid into a seat next to me on the bus. We chatted the whole way across the park, comparing our summer breaks and complaining about Mademoiselle Kiefer, our evil French teacher. When we got off on Broadway, Froggy said he had an hour to kill before his trombone lesson. I suggested we head over to my apartment and hang out.

I sounded innocent, but I have to admit I had ulterior motives with Froggy. Simply put, I was tired of being the only teenager in America—if not the world—who had yet to French-kiss. And along came Froggy, a halfway decent male specimen, with an hour to kill. The only trick was figuring out how to steer him from platonic-friend-who-hangs-out-and-watches-TV to lusty-guy-deflowering-my-virginal-kissing-status.

Opportunity knocked when we stepped into the elevator of my building. As I pushed the PH button, Froggy jokingly said, "So ... you live in the penthouse."

Thank you, *Penthouse*! The raunchy magazine that features naked vixens with basketball-sized boobs and skin oilier than a Pizza Hut pizza often gives people the wrong impression about my family's abode. A penthouse, in real life, is just the top floor of a building.

I shot Froggy a coy glance. "You know what they say about a girl who lives in a penthouse?"

It was an early September afternoon, particularly muggy in the elevator. Froggy grinned as he wiped the perspiration from his forehead. I felt a tremor deep in my gut, in that region south of my bellybutton.

As soon as we got into the apartment, I poured us both a tall glass of Diet Pepsi and we retreated to my bedroom. From there, it didn't take long—fourteen minutes, to be exact—until Froggy and I were making out.

Here's how it happened:

I said that the soda was making my braces cold. As I've read in myriad magazines, women should always call attention to their mouths, as in licking a lollipop or sliding on lip-gloss.

Froggy bought it hook, line, and sinker—going so far as to reach over and touch my brackets.

Once our faces were in such close proximity, we had no choice but to giggle and nuzzle noses and kiss.

 10

At first, it was nice. Nibbly and soft and not too spitty. I liked the way Froggy smelled up close, sort of sweet and musky and boyish.

But then I started worrying. *Does my inexperience show? What do I do with my tongue once it's in his mouth? Am I suctioning my lips too tightly? Should I keep my eyes open? Too weird! Or closed? Maybe. But what if HIS eyes are open and mine are closed and I make a freaky face and he sees it and laughs so hard that he bites off my tongue?*

I tried to recall make-out tips I've read, but then I remembered this quiz in a teen magazine where you rate your kissability on a scale of one to ten. I decided that I probably ranked about a two, maybe two and a half.

Froggy and I kissed for the next few minutes, until he glanced at my clock and dashed into the hallway to retrieve his trombone case.

Which brings us to today, two Mondays later, sprawled on my bedroom floor yet again. Froggy has spent the past several minutes fumbling around my shoulder blades. I don't have the guts to inform him that this particular bra unhooks in the front.

I'm doing my best imitation of a lover seized by passion. Eyelids heavy, faint upward curve to lips—just like women in movies who always look so orgasmic. But, truth be told, I'm having a

11

complete panic attack. I'm worried that Froggy is going to attempt to take off my shirt. It's OK for his hands to be rummaging *inside* it, but there's no way I'm letting him see my upper arms and stomach. I don't know where "*love* handles" got their name, but I have a feeling Froggy wouldn't find mine all that endearing.

I'm also double-checking and triple-checking whether I've locked my bedroom door. My workaholic parents rarely leave their offices before seven, and most nights they eat dinner out or grab something on the run. But I'd hate this to be the day they come home early, only to discover their youngest child going at it with a guy named after an amphibian.

I'm also trying to figure out why the droopy-eyed-faintly-smiling movie stars never mention rug burn. I have a plush pink carpet, but it's chafing my back every time my shirt slides up. I clutch both hands to the bottom of my shirt, anchoring it down. That serves the double purpose of not exposing any flabby body parts.

"Don't you want to…?" Froggy's voice cracks as he gestures in the direction of my boobs.

"That's not it." I point to the clock on my dresser. "It's just, you know, your trombone lesson."

Froggy tries to smooth back his hair, but it flops messily over his forehead. I'm tempted to run my fingers through his cowlick, but I know I shouldn't. No affectionate girlfriend-isms, especially once the make-out session has ended.

I escort Froggy to the front door, where he collects his backpack and trombone case from our foyer. I make a mental note to be more careful next time, to suggest that Froggy stash his stuff in my bedroom, just in case Mom or Dad or even my big brother makes a surprise visit. If there *is* a next time. I can never tell for sure.

Froggy stands in the doorway, rubbing his nose and pivoting his leg from side to side, like he's trying to burrow through the floor with his heel.

"Well, thanks," he says. "I'll see you in school."

"Yeah." I smile weakly and my lower lip gets snagged on my braces.

"Yeah," Froggy mumbles.

I try to muster the courage to suggest we sit together at lunch sometime, but then I wimp out, say one final *yeah*, and close the door.

CHAPTER TWO

About a year ago, before my sister joined the Peace Corps and moved to Africa, she sat me down and had a sex talk.

"Look," Anaïs said, flopping next to me on the couch. "I know Mom's not going to discuss this with you and I'd shudder to think what Dad would say, so I propose we have a little sex talk."

It was a quiet Saturday afternoon. Mom, Dad, and our brother, Byron, were at Yankee Stadium. I'd begged to go with them since they had four field-level seats, which would have offered prime views of players' butts in tight uniforms. But Byron made a case to bring his girlfriend du jour, a Parisian student who'd never seen a ball game before. Byron, a top debater in college, won out. Especially since my only argument was that I wanted to salivate over a certain sexy green-eyed shortstop.

 14

After they left, I spent an hour sulking—channel surfing, Web surfing, cupboard surfing—and basically feeling sorry for myself. Then I headed out to the street and bought the new *Teen People*, some Doritos, and a Snickers bar. When I got back to the apartment, I parked on the couch and devoured my magazine and my munchies until my sister interrupted me with the sex-talk business.

I wiped my Dorito-orange fingers on a paper towel and rolled my eyes. "I know about sex, if that's what you're wondering," I told Anaïs. "I've known for years."

"But do you know about guys?"

I stared at my sister.

"Right," she said. Then she launched into one of her rants, something she'd been doing ever since she discovered the feminist rocker Ani DiFranco and stopped shaving her legs. "Let me guess. On your thirteenth birthday, Mom left *It's Perfectly Normal* on your bed with a note that said"—Anaïs crooked her fingers like quotation marks—"'Come to me with questions.' But then, of course, she never has a spare minute to talk because she's too busy helping other teenagers figure things out and, anyway, who wants sex advice from someone who considers *Dad* an ideal mate?"

My jaw dropped to the floor. Mom is an adolescent psychologist here in New York City. She has a booming therapy practice and often speaks at conferences on teenagers. Dad is a high-pow-ered software executive. He's always going on business trips to Europe and California. One time he got written up in *Wired* for this digital music technology that his company engineered.

Even though they're in their early fifties, my par-ents are youngish-looking and active. Mom is a workout fiend. Dad is more of the sports-fan type. On warm weekends they go golfing together at their country club out in Connecticut. That's where Mom and Dad spend practically every weekend. We have a house in southwestern Connecticut. I used to go more when I was younger, but there's nothing to do out there—no TV, no high-speed connection, no town within walking distance—so I usually stay in the city on weekends.

"How did you know about *It's Perfectly Normal?*" I asked. That's the sexual health book that Mom gave me when I turned thirteen.

"She did the same for me." Anaïs twisted her curly dark hair into a knot on the top of her head. "But by the time she gave me *It's Perfectly Normal*, I'd already gotten my period, been felt up by two boys, and read every sexuality book in her study, all of which went typically"—Anaïs made the quo-tation marks again—"'unnoticed' by Mom."

"Well, you know how hard Mom works," I said. "She's totally overwhelmed by her—"

"Her patients? Her step-aerobics classes? Her

 16

social engagements?" Anaïs paused for a second and then sourly added, "Then again, when you're Dr. Phyllis Shreves, you don't have to worry about your *own* children because they're obviously going to turn out perfect *and* normal."

Dr. Phyllis Shreves. That's what Anaïs calls Mom whenever she's pissed at her. They argued a lot during my sister's senior year in college, about her decision to join the Peace Corps rather than go right to medical school. It always made me uncomfortable when they battled it out. I love my sister, but Mom usually knows what she's talking about when it comes to life plans.

I hugged a couch pillow to my stomach and attempted to change the subject. "Do you think Mom gave that book to Byron, too?"

Anaïs snorted. Anaïs snorts about anything related to our brother, who is four years older than me, four years younger than her. Anaïs is the only person I know who snorts in reference to Byron. The rest of the world worships him, myself included. He's incredibly handsome—supposedly the spitting image of Dad when he was in college— with tousled brown hair, maple-syrup-colored eyes, and a confident Shreves jaw. At that point, last summer, he was about to start Columbia, the Ivy League university here in New York City. Now he's in his sophomore year, where he's a star of the debate team, a rugby god, a total Don Juan lover-boy, and a straight-A student. Byron happens to think a lot of himself, but if I were even a smidgen like him, I'd have an ego the size of Brazil.

"I think she left Byron up to Dad. Can't you picture it?" Anaïs lowered her voice and scratched her chin mannishly. "You need sex ed, son? Here's a pack of condoms. Go out and get some."

I cracked up at my sister's imitation of Dad, which made me start choking on the sharp point of a Dorito. Anaïs shook her hair around her bare shoulders. She always wears skimpy tank tops and short shorts, things I could *never* imagine wearing, not even on the hottest days of summer. The best way to garb my heavier-than-average body is to hide it beneath layers of loose clothing. Mom's good at helping me pick out clothes that'll hide my weight. When the time comes for college, I'm considering checking out campuses in the Arctic Circle, where floor-length puffy coats are probably all the rage.

"Anyway, where were we?" Anaïs asked.

"The sex talk," I said, clearing my throat.

"Right."

Anaïs scooped up a handful of Doritos and briefed me on lust and crushes. She emphasized the importance of knowing your body, knowing what you like, because horny teenage guys aren't going to try to figure that out. She explained that, contrary to everything you see in movies, losing

 18

your virginity is sloppy and painful and about as fun as getting your toe amputated, so it should definitely happen with someone you care about.

We chatted on the couch until Mom, Dad, Byron, and the French girl returned from the ball game, giddy from beer, sunburns, and a Yankee victory. Mom's always nagging me about junk food, so I stashed the Doritos bag behind a couch cushion and buried my nose in *Teen People*. Anaïs retreated to her room, closed her door, and pumped an Ani album.

Three weeks later my sister began her two-year Peace Corps stint in Burkina Faso, where she's administering medication to impoverished West Africans.

And now, over a year later, as I stand in the hallway and stare at the door through which Froggy has just disappeared, I remember what Anaïs told me that afternoon.

"If you can't talk about something with a guy, you have no business doing it with him."

"You mean sex?" I asked.

"I mean anything. Making out. Second base. Third base. And, yes, home runs."

It made sense at the time. But now it dawns on me that it's easy for Anaïs to give that kind of advice when she's waify and gorgeous and people have stopped her on the sidewalk to tell her she should be a model.

When it comes to me, however, Anaïs failed to factor in one crucial thing. She forgot about the Fat Girl Code of Conduct.

CHAPTER THREE

I hear the elevator doors close, transporting Froggy down to the lobby. I head into the kitchen and splash my face with cool water. My cheeks feel feverish, so I lean into the spray for a long time. I use this sink as much as possible because the kitchen is the only room in the apartment besides mine that doesn't have a mirror. I hate mirrors. That's why I limit my reflection gazing to twelve seconds in the morning when I deal with my shoulder-length layered hair.

I've been mulling over the Fat Girl Code of Conduct a lot recently. Ever since I heard this joke on some creepy radio talk show as I was cruising the stations. Here's how it went:

Question: What do a fat girl and a moped have in common?

Answer: They're both fun to ride, as long as

your friends don't see you.

Really hilarious. So hilarious that it made me want to throw myself down our garbage chute, if only I could squeeze through the hole.

The strange thing is, as cruel as it was, that joke actually got me thinking. Basically, I can't resolve two contradictory facts of life.

Fact of Life: Fat girls don't get much action.
Fact of Life: I want to increase my kissability.

It's probably time to write a list. That's what I do whenever I'm overwhelmed and confused. It's not like I figure out any huge answers, but I always feel much better after my thoughts are in writing.

I dry my face with a paper towel and grab a handful of animal crackers. Once I'm in my bedroom, I switch on my computer, munch on two lions, and start writing.

The Fat Girl Code of Conduct
by Virginia Shreves

1. Any sexual activity is a secret. No public displays of affection. No air-kisses blown across the cafeteria. No carefully folded notes passed in the hall. No riding the moped in public.
2. Don't discuss your weight with him. Let's face it. You both know it's there, so don't start bemoaning your body and pressure him into lying, i.e., "What are you talking about? You don't look fat at all."

22

3. Go further than skinny girls. Find ways to alert him to this, such as slutty comments peppered into the conversation. If you can't sell him on your body, you'd better overcompensate with sexual perks.
4. Never, ever, ever, ever, ever push the relationship thing. Everybody knows that guys hate discussing relationships, so make it easy on him. Same goes for dates to movies and school dances. Bottom line: Let him get the milk without having to buy the cow.

I don't candy-coat my lists, so they tend toward the brutally honest. That's why I've never shown them to anyone, not even my best friend, Shannon. But I keep everything under password on my computer, just in case my family decides to poke around in my personal files.

To be honest, it's probably not necessary. I don't get the sense any of them are that interested in what's going on in my life, much less my head. Sometimes it feels like they don't think anything's going on at all.

I have this theory that I was switched at birth.

It doesn't happen much, but every once in a while you hear about a nutty hospital worker who swaps ID bracelets on two wailing infants.

I just know there's a stout, blond family out there, wondering how they wound up with a beautiful, slim, brown-haired daughter. What they don't realize is that she was meant to bear the name Virginia Shreves and live with her beautiful, slim, brown-haired family in a roomy apartment on Riverside Drive.

And I know that my beautiful, slim, brown-haired family wonders how they wound up with a daughter who has dishwater blond hair, pale blue eyes, a roundish face, and a larger-than-average body.

OK, fat.

Not *fat* fat. More like chubby fat.

Enough so I'm picked last in gym if the activity has anything to do with running, climbing ropes, or propelling oneself over a horse. Enough so I've heard people refer to me as plump, as if being likened to a vine-ripe tomato is some kind of compliment. Enough so family friends, upon comparing me to my skinny siblings, raise their eyebrows as high as McDonald's golden arches.

That's the most frustrating thing. I can't even blame it on genetics. Byron and Anaïs can eat whatever they want and still maintain their long, lanky bodies, just like Dad. If I so much as *smell* a bucket of fried chicken, I gain five pounds. I have more of Mom's metabolism. She used to be heavy when she was younger. She doesn't talk much about that time in her life. It's just occasional mentions of an awful childhood, a crazy family, how lucky we have it, how far she's come from Ozark,

Arkansas. Mom slimmed down by the time she went to Dartmouth and met Dad because in early pictures of them together, she looks about the same size as she is now.

Even so, she's always obsessing about not gaining weight again. She eats lettuce at every meal and spends half her life at the gym. I don't know what she's worried about because she's totally thin. Maybe it's Dad. He's the first to admit that he likes women skinny.

They say that people become shrinks to figure out their lives. That's probably the case with Mom. As soon as she hit college, she began studying adolescent psychology and didn't stop until she had a PhD. I think it would be interesting to do what Mom does, sit there all day and listen to teenagers spill their secrets. Dad shudders at the idea, but he's not happy unless he's managing dozens of people—phones ringing, beepers beeping, constant chaos. Byron and Anaïs are more like Dad that way. I'm more like Mom, craving plenty of peace and quiet.

That's probably why Mom reads so much. Whenever she's not working or working out, she's devouring a book. She named us after famous authors —Anaïs Nin, Lord Byron, Virginia Woolf—with the hope that we'd achieve greatness someday.

Except for my sister going into the Peace Corps, Anaïs and Byron have fulfilled all of Mom's dreams for her children. They are athletic and attractive. They love golfing at the country club in Connecticut. Our storage space in the basement is a treasure trove of their trophies and plaques and awards. They are both fluent in French, like my parents. Sometimes the four of them carry on an entire conversation in French. Anaïs also speaks Spanish and Byron is currently learning Japanese.

They all love artsy films. And jazz clubs. And museum exhibits. When she was in college, Anaïs brought home boyfriends with whom Dad shared his latest technology gadgets. Byron's girlfriends always bond with Mom, chatting it up about anything from StairMasters to Stella McCartney.

Sometimes I wonder if my parents wish they'd stopped at two kids. No one's ever spelled it out, but I think I was a mistake. They had me when they were in their late thirties, once they already had the ideal nuclear setup. And along came me, blemishing the image of a picture-perfect family.

I'm not saying I'm a huge loser. It's just that I'm not exceptional like the rest of them. I consume magazines at the speed of light. I love chatrooms and e-mail and instant messaging. I hate cardio-vascular exercise. I can't see the point in hitting a golf ball from here to eternity. I suck at French, but other than that I'm a pretty good student. I love sitcoms and reality shows and cheesy blockbuster movies. I'm not crazy about artsy films (they don't star anyone cute!) or jazz (no lyrics!) or museum exhibits (all the artists are dead!). Needless to say, a guy will probably never like me enough to want to meet my parents.

I'm definitely the weakest link in the Shreves clan.

I know I'm lucky to have been switched into such a stellar family. I just wish I made them feel more fortunate to have wound up with me.

CHAPTER FOUR

I'm standing at the entrance to the lunchroom, balancing a tray in my hands. The odor of burnt chicken nuggets and sour chocolate milk penetrates my nostrils. I feel like I'm going to puke, but I'm not sure if it's from the cafeteria stench or the anxiety in my stomach.

This is the moment I most dread every day. Back when Shannon was here, lunch was no big deal. We'd grab a table in the back and talk and laugh like we were the only people on the planet. But so far this year, it's been a panicky occasion. I never know who I'm going to sit with—or if I'll sit with anyone. Usually, I can locate some nice quiet types from one of my classes. But it's never consistent. And if one of my standby tables is full, I don't have a backup plan.

No, actually, here's my backup plan:

 28

I spend lunch period locked in a stall in the second-floor bathroom, eating Twinkies and flipping through magazines. It sounds gross, but it's actually OK. Especially since they installed toilet-seat lids over the summer, so it's not like I'm sitting over the open hole. No one really comes into that bathroom during lunch, so it's pretty peaceful. And they clean it on a regular basis, so it either smells like lemon-lime or bubble gum, depending on which cleanser the night-time janitor used.

It's not ideal. But no one ever said high school is a bed of roses.

My number-one objective in the lunchroom scenario is to not spend too much time hovering with my tray, gawking at my sea of classmates. It's essential to appear as if I know exactly where I'm sitting, which requires split-second scanning skills as I emerge from the food line and enter the cafeteria.

I hate calling attention to myself. A lot of it has to do with being heavy at a school where nearly every other girl weighs two pounds. Also, the cliques at Brewster are divided into popular, regular, and dorky—as kids refer to the various crowds. There's an unspoken rule that if you're not on the popular side of things, you shouldn't take up too much space. Just go with the flow and people will pretty much leave you alone.

29

If I had to chart it, I probably fall somewhere between regular and dorky.

I figure everyone starts with a zero and points are added or subtracted according to coolness/dorkyness.

I gain points because
- Byron went to school here and he was popular, so his legacy gives me some mileage (+5).
- I have decent hair that requires little work (+2).
- I'm smart, except in French (+2.5).

I lose points because
- I'm overweight (-6.5).
- I wear neutral colors, no sparkles, baggy khakis, oversize sweaters (-4).
- I'm smart, which works against you if you're smarter than a popular kid (-2).

On the far end of the cafeteria, I spot an available seat at a table of girls from my chemistry lab. The only problem is, Froggy Welsh the Fourth and his friends are at a neighboring table. Froggy and I haven't spoken since he was at my apartment two

 30

days ago, so I don't want to give him the wrong idea, like I'm stalking him.

I hear someone calling my name. I look over to see Ms. Crowley waving and heading my way.

"Virginia!" She squeezes my shoulder. "I've been hoping to run into you since the beginning of school."

Eileen Crowley was my ninth-grade language arts teacher. She's in her late thirties, a published poet, and moderately overweight. Some of the popular kids used to call her Ms. *Cow*ley behind her back, which made me so angry I would dig my fingernails into the palms of my hands. In my end-of-year evaluation letter, Ms. Crowley wrote: *It's rare to encounter a student like Virginia Shreves. What a talented writer! She'll go far.* I tucked that letter into the small cedar box that I keep in the back of my undies drawer. The only other things I have in that box are a strip of pictures Byron and I took in a photo booth at Grand Central Station, a MetroCard I once saw Ben Stiller drop on Broadway, and a snippet of Shannon's red hair.

Ms. Crowley must have read my mind. "I've been wondering how you're surviving without your spiritual twin."

"Shannon?" I ask, readjusting the tray in my hands.

Ms. Crowley nods.

"It's definitely different with her away," I say.

31

I guess I'd call Shannon my spiritual twin. She's my best friend. Her full name is Shannon Iris Malloy-Newman. I've heard people describe her as mousy, but I firmly believe she was a cat in a former life. She's small and graceful, with pumpkin-colored hair, masses of freckles, and feline-like eyes. She's incredibly funny, but most people don't give her the chance to show it. Shannon has a stutter, so it can take her several tries to complete a sentence. She rarely stutters around me. Only with strangers or during a class presentation or if she's trying to say something quickly. Sometimes I think our handicaps (me = heavy; Shannon = stutter) are what initially brought us together, back in sixth grade. From there, we totally connected.

Shannon is away for the school year. In Walla Walla, Washington. I once joked that Walla Walla is a haven for stutterers because it's one of the only geographic locations where you're *supposed* to say the name twice.

"Great, Virginia," Shannon had responded. "A town full of stutterers with bad breath. *Just perfect.*"

Walla Walla is the hometown of the Walla Walla onion. That's what brought Shannon's family to Walla Walla. Shannon's dad is writing a book on onions. Liam Newman always writes about obscure topics, like the role of the shoelace throughout history, which was a bestseller in New Zealand.

 32

But onions. Onions are the clincher.

Appropriate topic, actually, because whenever I think about facing the next ten months without Shannon, I burst into tears.

Ms. Crowley must sense something on my face. "Virginia, are you ever free during lunch period?"

"Sure ... why?"

"I'm swamped with grading my freshman vocabulary tests. Remember how many I gave you last year?"

I nod.

"I'd love your help," she says.

"Really?"

"My office is still on the second floor. Come up anytime. I'm always there this period."

As soon as Ms. Crowley is out of sight, I glance down at my tray. The side dish of corn has congealed, so little blobs of butter are mingling with the bloated kernels. I grab the Twinkies and toss the rest of my lunch into the trash bin. As I do, I notice Froggy looking my way. I think he's smiling, so I offer a brief smile back. Enough so he'll see it, but not so much that I'll look like a freak grinning into thin air.

Then I hurry out of the cafeteria and head up the stairs to spend the rest of the period in peace.

Ten minutes later I'm locked in a stall, flipping through *Seventeen*, when I hear the bathroom door open and some pairs of shoes click in.

I breathe a sigh of relief that I'm far from the mirrors, where the feet are remaining. But as I peek through the crack between the doorway and stall, I groan to myself.

It's Brie Newhart, Brinna Livingston, and Briar Schwartz. The Queen Bee Popular Girls of the tenth grade. Major requirements: be bony, be bitchy, and begin your name with "Bri." Brinna and Briar are Ladies in Waiting, actually. Brie is the head honcho. Never mind the fact that she's named after a fattening French cheese, she's as skinny as an eight-year-old boy. She's also gorgeous, with wide blue eyes, sandy-brown curls, and Neutrogena-model skin. Supposedly her family is loaded, so she can have anything she wants. Even so, she wears the same high-heeled magenta boots every day. I overheard her say she got them in Paris over the summer. To top it off, Brie has a sweet voice and a toothpaste-model smile, so teachers go gaga over her.

Brie and her friends are in a completely different stratosphere than I am, so it's not like I ever talk to them. But sometimes I watch Brie across a classroom and wonder how one single person can be endowed with so many gifts. I inch my legs up, so I'm sitting cross-legged on the toilet seat, clutch my magazine, and breathe as quietly as humanly possible.

I can see them through the crack. They're

clustered around the wide mirror, unclasping their little black bags and producing various lip and eye products. I half listen to them discussing makeup, shopping, body, hair, body, shopping, makeup.

Brinna brags about how little she ate yesterday, something about one peeled cucumber and a bag of Veggie Booty.

Briar boasts about spending two hours at the gym last night.

Brie, of course, tops them both.

"I was at French Connection and I didn't even fit into their size-two skirts." She pauses before adding, "*Trop grande.*" I think Brie is saying "too big" in French.

"Oh my god!" squeals Brinna.

"I'm *so* jealous!" says Briar.

Then they start talking about guys. Brinna and Briar go back and forth about which seniors are hot. Brie cluck-clucks at their choices, saying that she finds any guy under eighteen completely *boooring*.

"Speaking of older men," Brie says, "guess who I ran into on the subway last weekend?"

"Who?" Brinna and Briar ask.

"Remember Byron Shreves? He was a senior when we were in eighth grade."

I can't believe this! I hold my breath and wait to hear what the others say.

"Oh my god!" squeals Brinna.

"He was *so* sexy!" says Briar.

"Well, you should see him now," says Brie. "*Oooh la la!* He's a sophomore at Columbia and totally filled out. We flirted for four stops on the local train."

As Briar and Brinna *oooh* and *aaah* and *oh my god*, I begin to relax. But then I hear something that makes my stomach lurch.

"Doesn't his sister go to Brewster?" Brinna asks.

"Yeah," says Briar. "Virginia."

"Virginia *who*?" asks Brie.

Ouch. I know Brie and I reside in different universes, but still. We've been going to Brewster since sixth grade. And we're in three classes together, for god's sake.

"Virginia Shreves," says Briar, cracking up. "That chubby girl."

"No way!" Brie shrieks. "I never knew they were related."

"Of course they are," says Briar. "It's not like Shreves is a common name."

I bite down on the flesh inside my cheeks. *That chubby girl.*

After a moment Brie says, "All I can say is, if I were that fat, I'd kill myself."

"Totally," murmur Briar and Brinna in unison.

When the bell rings a few minutes later, the Bri-girls—who'd long since changed the subject—file out of the bathroom. I remain locked in my stall, gnawing at my cheeks. My spit tastes salty from the swirls of blood. I can feel loose flaps of skin with my tongue.

I can't get those words out of my head.

Brie and Brinna and Briar would rather be dead than be me.

CHAPTER FIVE

I'm still feeling crappy on the bus ride home from school. I can't stop thinking about what Brie said. I've been teased a lot in my life, especially in junior high, when kids oinked at me in the halls or asked if I was pregnant when I was wearing a loose dress. But there's something particularly dreadful about *overhearing* people trash you.

As I trudge through the lobby, the doorman hands me a package wrapped in brown paper and covered with stickers. I glance at the return address. *Shannon Iris Malloy-Newman.* I love presents, especially ones from my best friend, so it lifts my spirits a little.

When I arrive in our apartment, I go right to the freezer and pull out a Popsicle. The ice cream soothes the insides of my cheeks, which are raw and sore. Mom's always insisting we only have healthy foods in the kitchen, but Dad has a sweet tooth, so he manages to smuggle home the good stuff.

As soon as I'm in my bedroom, I tear open Shannon's package. Underneath the brown-bag exterior is a smaller parcel wrapped in tissue paper. I rip off the paper and crack up. Shannon has sent me a green sweatshirt that says WALLA WALLA IS FOR LOVERS on the front. It's fuzzy on the inside and extra-extra-large, just the way I like it.

I'm slipping the sweatshirt over my head when the door opens and Byron steps into my room. I've told him a million times to knock first, but he never seems to remember.

I'm not surprised to see Byron. His dorm is only forty blocks from our apartment, so he often drops by to do his laundry or loot the cupboards. But today he's wearing a starched white shirt and tuxedo pants. He's still barefoot, though. I notice patches of hair sprouting up from his big toes.

"Hey, Gin," Byron says. "Would you help me with these cuff links?"

"Sure."

As I fasten on the silver cuff links, I can't stop thinking about how he flirted with Brie Newhart on the subway a few days ago. I'm tempted to tell him what a bitch she is and that the next time he sees her he should shove her in front of an oncoming train. But I can't. Because then I'd have to tell him what she said and I can't tell anyone that. Not ever.

"Why are you all dressed up?" I ask.

"Mom invited me to some fancy dinner. Lots of big-time shrinks will be there. Should be interesting."

Dad hates wearing tuxedos, so Mom is always bringing Byron to black-tie events. She used to do the same with Anaïs. I keep hoping Mom will invite me one of these days, but she hasn't so far.

As soon as I've finished with his cuff links, Byron runs his fingers through his wet hair. "Does your big brother clean up nicely or what?"

"You look great," I say. I quickly glance at his chest, to see if it's true what Brie said. He looks a little bigger, more filled out. He spent all summer lifting weights, so I guess it's starting to pay off.

"After jeans and sweatshirts on campus every day," Byron says, "it feels so civilized to dress up."

"Speaking of sweatshirts, what do you think? Shannon just mailed it to me."

Byron studies my sweatshirt. "I don't get it."

"What's there to get?"

"It's a little silly. I mean, *Paris* is for lovers, not Walla Walla."

I roll my eyes. "That's the irony, stupid."

"Couldn't she have gotten a smaller size?" Byron asks.

"What do you mean?"

"That one's just so..." Byron searches for the

right word. "Extra-large."

Extra-large. I can feel the tears coming on. *Virginia who? That chubby girl.* I choke out a quick laugh and tell Byron I have homework to do.

Once he's gone, I yank off the sweatshirt and kick it under my bed, so it's mingling with the dust balls and Jolly Rancher wrappers that the vacuum cleaner never seems to reach.

To: goddess_shannon
From: citigurl13
Date: Wednesday, September 25, 4:38 p.m.
Subject: extra-large

Shannon—

I just got your sweatshirt in the mail. I'd vowed to wear it every single day until you return home, but then Byron told me it looked extra-large. Which means, of course, that he's talking about ME and the fact that I LOOK extra-large in it. Which is probably true. No, I bet I look FAT. Because I am. I'm fat and repulsive and should live among the blind for the remainder of my days.

I'm sorry to sound so down.

I love the sweatshirt.

It's just me that I hate.

Virginia

"Don't *you* look handsome!" I hear Mom exclaim.

"I can't get my bow tie straight," says Byron. "Can you help me with it?"

"Sure, honey. Just let me set down my..."

As their voices fade, I stretch out across my comforter. I'm on my bed reading *People* and trying to clear my mind. Mom thinks tabloid magazines are a waste of time, but a good dose of celebrity gossip always helps me forget my own problems.

There's a knock on my door.

I shove *People* under my pillow and stick my nose in *The Scarlet Letter*. That's what we're reading for language arts right now. We're doing a unit this fall called "Ostracism and Oppression." I actually like *The Scarlet Letter*. It's about a woman in colonial New England who committed adultery, so the Puritanical townspeople force her to wear an embroidered red "A" on her chest as a punishment for her sin. Bizarre, but interesting.

"Yeah?" I ask.

Mom peeks inside.

"You're home early," I say.

"I rescheduled some patients so I could get ready for tonight." Mom twirls around the center of my room. "What do you think?"

"About what?"

"My hair. I just got the color touched up."

Mom's hair is naturally dirty blond, like mine,

42

but she always has her colorist add chestnut streaks.

I shrug. "It looks nice."

"Well, it's a professional expense."

That's how Mom justifies treating herself to facials, expensive shoes, silk scarves. She gives the receipts to her accountant, who writes them off as professional expenses. Dad's always saying that we're doing fine and Mom doesn't have to justify her luxury items. But Mom grew up on the verge of poverty, so it's difficult for her to spend money without major guilt.

Mom is so together that it's hard to imagine she used to be Phyllis Nutford, Fat Girl from Ozark, Arkansas. Her classmates used to call her Phyllis *Nutcase*. I only know this because I once discovered her old yearbooks stashed in our storage space in the basement. I also learned that her high school's mascot was the hillbilly. No joke. Barefoot, overalls, a corncob pipe, the whole bit. Mom would murder me if she knew I looked through her yearbooks. She wants to put as much distance as possible between her Ozark past and her Manhattan present. She barely even stays in touch with the Nutty Nutfords. I've only met that side of the family once, when I was nine and they were in town for a dog competition. I have to say, they were definitely up there with cashews and pistachios.

"Mom?"

"Yes?"

"Why can't I ever go to these events with you?"

Mom clicks her manicured fingers up and down my keyboard. "You will."

I sit up. "Really?"

"Sure."

"Do you have any idea when?"

"I can't give you an exact date, Virginia," Mom says. Then she pauses and adds, "I just wanted to tell you that I made an appointment for you with a new doctor. It's next Monday afternoon. I'll meet you here and we can take a cab up there together."

"Why do I need a new doctor?" I ask. "What's wrong with Dr. Nakamura?"

Dr. Nakamura is my pediatrician. I've been going to her since I was three.

"This guy specializes in adolescent medicine," Mom says. "I heard about him through some colleagues. He's all the way up at Columbia Presbyterian, but I think it'll be worth it for you to see him."

"Why?" I ask. "I feel fine."

Mom gets an uncomfortable look on her face. I know what's coming next. It's about my weight. Mom has a hard time talking about my body. Her shrink side wants to reassure me that I'm fine the way I am, accept myself, all that self-esteem stuff.

44

But her Mom side wants me to be thin and perfect, like the rest of the Shreves. The end result is that she can barely say the word "fat" around me. She uses euphemisms such as "heavy" and "like I used to be."

After a moment Mom says, "I want to discuss your nutrition with the new doctor."

"My nutrition?" I ask. "Why can't I see Nan again?"

Nan Grossman is a friend of Mom's from the gym. I privately called her Nan the Neurotic Nutritionist because she's always freaking out about additives and preservatives and caloric content.

Mom sighs impatiently. "Look, I've got to start getting ready for tonight. Just remember ... Monday at four-thirty."

"Fine," I say. I lean against my pillow and pick up *The Scarlet Letter*.

I know Mom's intentions are good, like she wants to help me feel better and look better and be a better person. But I can't help wishing she accepted me the way I am. And I can't help wondering whether if I were thin, I'd get invited to these fancy dinners as well.

As soon as Mom is gone, I grab *People* out from under my pillow and immerse myself in a scintillating story about collagen lips.

*　　*　　*

Mom said that Dad would be home around seven, but I don't hear from him until eight, when he calls from his cell phone.

"I'm picking up some Chinese food," he says. "What would you like?"

"Nothing."

"Aren't you hungry?"

"Not really," I say. I don't mention that I've already eaten a heaping bowl of pasta, the leftover Vietnamese food from last night, and a container of cherry yogurt.

"Do you want an egg roll?"

"No, thanks."

"OK. I'll be home in ten minutes. Has the game started?"

"Just singing the National Anthem."

When Dad comes through the door, he's toting two plastic bags. I'm stretched on the couch, wrapped in a blanket and watching the ball game.

"Score?" he shouts as he heads into the kitchen.

"One–nothing, Yankees."

"Inning?"

"Top of the second."

When Dad joins me a few minutes later, he's carrying a glass of wine and a plate overflowing with shrimp, asparagus, and rice. He sits on the ottoman and spreads a checkered dishtowel across his lap.

"They're going to beat Boston, Ginny," Dad

 46

says as he sips his wine. "I can feel it in my bones."

"Me, too."

Dad and I both love the Yankees, though for different reasons. He wants to see them make it to the World Series. I want to bear their children. Whenever Dad is home, we watch the games together.

During a commercial Dad carries his dishes into the kitchen and returns with a plate heaped with pastries.

"I stopped by the bakery," Dad says, handing me a napkin. "Thought I'd pick up some treats."

I prop myself onto my elbows and eye a plump slice of apple strudel.

Dad drops two cookies onto his napkin. "Let's consider it a pre-celebration."

I sink my teeth into the strudel.

We've polished off all the pastries when a beer commercial comes on. A woman in microscopic shorts and a bikini top parades around the baseball diamond.

Dad whistles. "Now *there's* an attractive woman."

Typical Dad. He's constantly praising thin women's bodies. It used to drive Anaïs crazy. Whenever Dad complimented her figure, she would yell at him and spout feminist theory about how men shouldn't judge women by their body type. Even though I'm used to hearing the skinny-women-are-more-attractive spiel, it strikes a sore

47

nerve tonight.

I feel my stomach tightening up.

Nine hours ago, Brie Newhart said that if she were as fat as me, she'd kill herself.

Five hours ago, Byron called me extra-large.

Four hours ago, Mom announced that I have to see a special doctor about my "nutrition."

And here I am, wolfing down Popsicles and pasta and pastries.

To: citigurl13
From: goddess_shannon
Date: Wednesday, September 25, 9:58 p.m.
Subject: wallowing in walla walla

Virginia—

Duh! What a dumb thing for Byron to say! Why can't he be nice to you for a change?

Not much to report in Walla Walla. Liam and Nina are currently having a love affair with onions. It's all they talk about. And cook. French onion soup. Sausage and onions. They even baked an onion pie the other day. No wonder I'm not making any friends.

I'm counting the days until I return to NYC.

Love,
Shannon

P.S. 298. See? I really am counting.

To: goddess_shannon
From: citigurl13
Date: Wednesday, September 25, 10:11 p.m.
Subject: sucky solidarity

S—

It sucks here, too. At least we can be comforted by the fact that we are in sucky solidarity.

I can't write much because I've got to study for Friday's French quiz. Did you know that "fat" in French is "gros"? If I didn't hate French enough already, I hate it even more now.

V

P.S. Byron was just being honest.

CHAPTER SIX

"*Carry me back to old Virginny*," Mr. Moony sings as I approach his desk.

I hear a few kids in the study hall chuckling. I hug my notebooks to my chest and pray that my cheeks aren't too flushed or my butt doesn't look too big.

"*There's where the cotton and the corn and taters grow*," Mr. Moony warbles, tapping his worn leather shoe as he sings the old hymn about the state of Virginia.

Clive Moony is my geometry teacher and the oldest living person. He probably taught math when the abacus was the latest technology. He's so ancient that he's senile. He can never remember any mathematical formulas. But he's managed to retain a database of songs in his head, songs that have our first names in them, songs that he delights

 50

in singing to mortified students.

I generally try to avoid Mr. Moony. I never raise my hand in his class for fear of being serenaded. He's also my study hall teacher, so I rarely ask for a pass to the bathroom or the water fountain. But I've been languishing in study hall for the past twenty minutes. I've finished my homework and chewed off nine fingernails. If I have to listen to the buzz of the fluorescent lights for one more second, I'm going to gnaw off my left arm.

I finally reach Mr. Moony's desk. I hurriedly explain how I *must* go to the computer cluster to finish up a global studies assignment. Instead of simply filling out a hall pass, Mr. Moony responds with another song.

"Almost heaven, West Virginiaaaaaah…"

He pauses to suck in a raspy breath, so I quickly interject. "Could you *please* give me a pass to the computer cluster?"

Mr. Moony closes his eyes, sways his liver-splotched head from side to side, and continues crooning "Country Roads."

"TODAY!" I shout, surprising even myself.

Mr. Moony flaps open his droopy eyelids. "What did you want?"

"A pass." I gnaw off my final fingernail.

"Where?"

I clench my jaw. "To the computer cluster."

51

"Oh, sure," says Mr. Moony. "Why didn't you say so in the first place?"

The computer cluster is one of Brewster's favorite bragging points. It's a well-lit room on the ground floor. All of the school's promotional literature drones on about "state-of-the-art equipment that will situate every student on the cutting edge of contemporary technology." Translation: twenty computers, twenty ergonomic chairs, and a lot of Web surfing during free periods.

The room is more populated than usual. I hand my pass to Krishna. He's the NYU student who works part-time overseeing the computer cluster. He's a nice guy if you can look beyond his pockmarked skin and thrasher band T-shirts.

"Your favorite computer is still available," says Krishna, pointing to the tangerine-colored Macintosh in the back.

I glance at a group of guys clustered around the newest Mac. "What's going on?"

"They're fooling around with some graphic design program," says Krishna.

I study the jumble of baseball caps and skateboard duds and scuffed sneakers. I recognize several of the kids, fellow sophomores. And then, in the center of the action, there's Froggy Welsh the Fourth. He's leaning toward the monitor, one hand on the keyboard, the other gripping the mouse.

Oh god. Now Froggy's *totally* going to think I'm stalking him.

Krishna continues. "It's mostly the guy with the blond hair. What's his name? Frog?"

"Froggy," I say in a hushed voice.

"Yeah, Froggy. Supposedly, he's this huge graphic design whiz."

"Really?"

"They say he'll be a millionaire before he's twenty."

I peek over at Froggy. I wonder what he could ever see in me. He has his group of friends. He has his trombone. And now he's this budding computer genius, the next Bill Gates. The last thing I want to do is park my big butt at a neighboring computer, which would present two miserable, pathetic options:

Miserable, Pathetic Option #1: Froggy would feel sorry for me and give me a pity wave.

Miserable, Pathetic Option #2: Froggy would ignore me, making me feel like a loser with a capital "L."

I know about the Fat Girl Code of Conduct, but this whole ride-moped-in-private arrangement makes me feel awful sometimes. In movies people fool around without giving it a second thought, so I always thought it would be easy. But with Froggy, I'm getting a little attached. I mean, I can still feel his lips on my lips, his fingers stroking my cheeks.

So how can it be that four days later we barely say hello to each other? And, come Monday, we'll most likely be rolling on my rug again?

I need to get out of here. Normally I'd hide out in the second-floor bathroom, but I've been avoiding it ever since the Bri-girls episode. Then I remember Ms. Crowley's offer to help grade freshman vocabulary tests.

"Krishna?"

"Yeah?"

"Can you give me a pass to Ms. Crowley's office?"

I take the back staircase. Less chance of running into anyone as I huff to the second floor.

This is one of the many things I hate about Brewster. The thousands of stairs we must mount on a daily basis. There's actually a creaky elevator, but it's only used for carting desks and chairs and Mr. Moony. Students are expected to ascend multiple flights on an hourly basis without so much as leaking a drop of sweat. Because the Model Brewster Student is a lean, mean, stair-climbing machine.

That's another thing I hate about Brewster. The Model Brewster Student. They're always talking about the MBS at assemblies. They even give out MBS awards every fall. The MBS is "worldly and active and humanitarian," so they say. They also like to ramble on about how the MBS is "generous and kind, embodying the qualities

of our esteemed founder, Theodore Brewster."
The truth is, if you want to be an MBS, you
have to dress a certain way (preppy/urban/chic)
and look a certain way (white/skinny/flawless
skin). Except, of course, when Brewster is taking
pictures for their promotional booklets. Then the
MBS is black/Asian/Latino/Indian/biracial, but
still skinny and without a zit in sight.

It's all such a crock. First of all, Brie Newhart
won an MBS award last year, and she's definitely
not "generous and kind," at least not to the regular or dorky kids. But what's really ironic is that
Theo Brewster was a tough-talking rumrunner
during the Prohibition era of the 1920s. That's
how he made his fortune. He smuggled rum from
sugar cane plantations in the Caribbean to booze-
thirsty ports in the Northeast.

That's why every spring, on Brewster Day, they
serve us piña coladas and strawberry daiquiris, just
without the alcohol. The seniors sneak in miniature bottles of rum, spike their drinks, and spend
the rest of Brewster Day singing pirate songs.

At least that's what Byron told me happened
when he went to school here.

Ms. Crowley is standing behind her desk. Her
wavy hair is secured into a bun with two yellow
pencils. The wisps around her face are held back
by paper clips.

"Hello there," she says, smiling.

My heart is still thumping from taking the stairs two at a time. "I was just wondering if you needed help grading tests, like you said the other day."

Ms. Crowley glances at her watch. "I'm running out to a meeting, so I don't have time to get you started." She studies my face for a second before adding, "You can hang out here for the rest of the period, if you'd like."

I step into her office. "Are you sure?"

Ms. Crowley maneuvers around me. "Make yourself comfortable. Read whatever you want. My computer's still on, if you want to tool around."

"Thanks, Ms. Crowley." I set my notebooks on her desk.

"My pleasure." She hoists a tote bag onto her shoulder. "Let's do the tests another time."

As soon as she's gone, I sink into her chair and survey the small room. Ms. Crowley's office is cluttered with books and coffee mugs and photographs of her husband and their two Great Danes. The only other chair is piled high with literary journals. I think a few of them have published Ms. Crowley's poems. An entire section of her bookshelf is dedicated to poetry compilations by Maya Angelou, e.e. cummings, Allen Ginsberg, Pablo Neruda.

On a top shelf, I spot *A Room of One's Own* by

Virginia Woolf. I've tried reading several books by Virginia Woolf, since Mom named me after her and everything. But I always get lost after a few pages. Her writing is so dense and enigmatic. Exactly what you'd expect from someone who committed suicide by filling her pockets with stones and walking into a river.

I open my notebook to a fresh page and scribble *Froggy + Virginia*. It's strange to see it on paper. It makes me wish I could write it on my locker or with a highlighter on my hand, like other girls do with their crushes. I tear out the page, rip it to shreds, and sprinkle it into the trash can.

That's when I notice that Ms. Crowley's office overlooks the small courtyard behind the school. I've never actually set foot in there since that's where the popular kids sneak out to smoke cigarettes.

There are mostly juniors and seniors in the courtyard. And then I see Brie Newhart weaving through the crowd, sucking at a cigarette and flaunting her Parisian boots.

I turn away from the window, face Ms. Crowley's computer, and compose an e-mail to Shannon. I haven't heard from her in a few days. I hope she's not too miserable out there in Walla Walla.

I mention that there are only 296 days until our lives begin again.

I don't mention that it's lucky I'm not near a pile

of stones and the Hudson River.

Because I can't guarantee that if given the opportunity, I wouldn't take Brie's advice and go the way of my namesake.

CHAPTER SEVEN

On Saturday I sleep in until 11 A.M. Mom and Dad are long gone by the time I wake up. They always leave for Connecticut at the crack of dawn, so they can beat traffic and hit the golfing green early. Most weekends they don't return until Sunday evening. They call and check in a few times, but basically I have two solid days to myself.

When Anaïs was in college and Byron was fifteen or sixteen, weekends were great. As soon as Mom and Dad took off, my brother and I would take over the apartment. We'd keep the TV going for thirty-six hours. We didn't pick up our wet towels. We'd make kooky food creations. We wouldn't do a single dish until 5 P.M. on Sunday.

But then Byron got into girls and going out, so I began spending weekends at Shannon's apartment down in Greenwich Village. But with Shannon in Walla Walla, weekends have been a drag recently.

Dad's always saying, "Give Ginny a stack of magazines, a computer, and a TV and she's set for life."

I guess that's true. But even I get a little lonely sometimes.

I pour myself a bowl of Rice Krispies, plop onto the couch, and scan the movie listings. The pickings are sparse today, the highlight of the afternoon being *Babe: Pig in the City*, which they aired twice last weekend.

I know some families are all *rah-rah* about having nightly sit-down dinners. Believe me, it would be nice to have a Shreves family meal every once in a while, but I've basically come to accept that that's not what my family is about. Besides, Byron and I used to have a blast creating our own dishes. They were much better than stir-fry or spaghetti or whatever normal families eat every night.

Sometimes we'd make run-of-the-mill things like Rice Krispie treats, except we'd eat them for dinner, which rendered them exotic. One time, when I was sick, Byron made me a waffle sundae. He toasted an Eggo and topped it with vanilla ice cream and chocolate syrup. Making food together became our special ritual. Sometimes on a Saturday evening or a Sunday afternoon, as we were plugging away in the kitchen, I would get a warm feeling inside, wishing we could freeze the moment forever. Other times, I would have the craziest notions. Like hoping Mom and Dad would get into a car accident and Byron and I could live together, just the two of us.

But everything changed once my brother got popular. "In demand" is what Mom used to call it. He had dates with girls on weekend nights. And during the day he hung out with his friends at Chelsea Piers. That's around the time I started blimping out, so I think Byron got embarrassed to be seen with me in public. He never said as much, but sometimes it felt like he was walking a few strides ahead of me on the sidewalk.

I choke up as that thought crosses my mind.

I miss spending time with the old Byron. Maybe he misses it, too. Maybe he wants our closeness back, but he's too busy with school and life to do anything about it.

As I set my empty cereal bowl on the coffee table, I come up with a great idea. I race into the kitchen and tear through the cupboards to see what ingredients we have and what I need to go out and buy.

Two hours later I'm riding the subway up to Columbia, toting a warm batch of Rice Krispie treats topped with a melted layer of chocolate morsels. I'm hoping the goodies will jump-start

61

Byron's memory of the old days. If nothing else, it'll soften the shock of showing up, unannounced, at his dorm on a Saturday afternoon.

I've never dropped in on Byron at college before. I visited his old room a few times last year, with Mom and Dad. And then, in late August, we helped him move into his new suite. That was after my parents' Biannual Byron Brunch. At the beginning of every new semester, they put out a huge bagel spread and invite the whole world—from downstairs neighbors to Connecticut friends to Byron's preschool teacher. Everyone toasts Byron and, wired on coffee, the guests' speeches commending him last longer than the president's State of the Union address.

Byron's dorm is called Wallach. I thought I remembered where it was, but as I step through Columbia's entranceway, all the buildings look identical—stately, stone, draped in ivy. I stop a professor type on the path and ask him about Wallach. He gestures to a dorm off in the distance.

It's a balmy fall afternoon, so the grassy expanses in front of the majestic library are overflowing with students. Everyone is tossing Frisbees, stretched out on blankets, laughing, eating chips, writing in notebooks. I scan the crowd for Byron. I hadn't considered the fact that he might not be in his room. If he's not there, I guess I could just hang out in his hallway for a while. Either that or leave the treats at his door with a note to call me.

Once I get to Wallach, I spot a security guard at the front desk. She's checking everyone's student ID cards. I linger on the front steps until a gaggle of students filters into the dorm. As they hand their IDs to the guard, I slip past them and dash up the narrow staircase.

I mount three flights of stairs, catch my breath, and study doors until I find Byron's suite. That's just a fancy way of saying he's in a single room with several other singles, a shared bathroom, and a common room.

I cross the empty common room and knock on Byron's door.

"Door's open," he says.

I try the knob. It's locked, so I knock again.

"Door's open."

"It's not," I say. "I just tried it."

Silence.

"Virginia?" Byron asks.

"Yeah?"

Byron swings open the door. His hair is kind of messy and he's wearing shorts and a beat-up T-shirt that says COLUMBIA RUGBY.

"Hey," I say.

He looks like he doesn't know what to make of all this. "What are you doing here?"

I'm quiet for a second. This isn't how I imagined

63

it. Not that I pictured us throwing our arms around each other, but I thought maybe a "what a pleasant surprise" might be in order.

"I made you these." I open the Tupperware container and reveal the contents. "Thought you'd like them."

"Well," he says, rubbing his cheeks. "Well, well."

"Can I come in?"

Byron opens his door wider and I step into his room. The first thing I notice is that he's replaced the bed with a futon mattress directly on the gray industrial carpet. On the windowsill, there are three candles with frozen waterfalls of wax.

I kick off my shoes and sit on the futon. Byron settles into his chair. I offer him a Rice Krispie treat, but he shakes his head.

"What are you up to today?" I ask.

"Not much," Byron says. "Getting some reading done for a paper."

"Oh." I nibble some chocolate off a treat.

"How's Brewster?" Byron asks after a moment.

"Fine," I say. "Same as usual."

"Is Old Moony still there?"

"Yep," I say. "Still singing his crazy songs."

"He used to sing some to me," says Byron, "but they were always about *Brian* and I didn't have the heart to correct him."

We both laugh.

I polish off the rest of my treat.

There's a knock on the door.

"Come on in," Byron calls out.

The door opens to reveal a smallish guy with closely shorn hair and a pointy nose. He smiles as he eyes me on Byron's bed. Actually, not a smile. More of a male-bonding grin. If there could be a facial expression that conveyed a thumbs-up sign, this would be it.

"Never a surprise to see a lovely young woman hanging out in Lord Byron's room," he says. "Who have we got here?"

As much as I think incest is the grossest thing in the world, I'm flattered that someone would actually think Byron and I are enough in the same league to be "hanging out." Also, do I need my hearing checked or did this guy just call me "a lovely young woman"?

I'm totally basking in the praise, but Byron doesn't seem thrilled about the mix-up. "It's my little sister," he says, shooting the guy a scolding look. Then he nods in my direction. "This is Shawn. He lives in our suite."

"Hi, Little Sister," Shawn says. "Do you have a name?"

"Virginia." I pull one of Byron's pillows onto my lap. I always feel safer that way, like my body is more concealed.

"Virginia." Shawn lifts up a stapler and sets it

down again. His jerky movements remind me of a hamster. As he gives me the once-over, I hug the pillow tighter around my middle. "Are you *really* Byron's sister?"

"Yeah," I say.

Shawn glances from my brother to me and back again. "You're serious, man?" he asks Byron. "You two look nothing alike."

There's a long silence in which I can't help but wonder: Is it our hair color? I have a Yankee cap on. Our height? I'm sitting on the bed. Our weight? *Aha!*

Byron switches on his computer. "So, what's up?" he asks Shawn.

"Not much." Shawn picks some wax off one of the candles. "Just letting you know we're tapping the pre-party keg in the common room around ten."

"Sounds great," Byron says.

Shawn rolls the wax between his finger and thumb. "You're coming to Virgins and Sluts, aren't you?"

"Yep," says Byron.

"Are you still bringing Annie Mills?"

"Yep."

"Lord Byron strikes again," sings Shawn. "She's cute, man." Shawn rubs his knuckles up and down his chest. "For a math major."

As soon as Shawn is gone, I ask, "What's

 66

Virgins and Sluts?"

Byron enters his password into his computer. "That's this party that a bunch of us are going to tonight."

"Why is it called Virgins and Sluts?"

Byron takes a deep breath. "The theme is 'the more you bare, the less the fare.' The cover charge is ten bucks, but there's a sliding scale depending on how much skin you reveal."

"Who's Annie Mills?"

"Just a girl."

I scratch at a pimple on my arm. "Do you know what she's going to wear?"

Byron laughs. "She says she's wearing a black leather bustier and fishnets, but I'll believe it when I see it."

"What about you?"

"I don't know. Probably just boxers."

I examine my arm. A tiny dot of blood has cropped up, so I rub it off with my thumb.

We chat for a few more minutes. I eat a Rice Krispie treat and then another and then another, until I realize there are only five left in the Tupperware. Byron hasn't even had one, which strikes me as a little strange. This is the boy who used to consume an entire panful during the course of a half-hour sitcom.

After a while Byron stretches his arms over his head and yawns loudly. "I'd better get started on this paper," he says. "Fifteen pages. Due Wednesday."

"I hope you have fun tonight," I say.

I give Byron a meaningful stare. I guess on some small level, I'm hoping he'll invite me to hang out for the rest of the afternoon, maybe go with him and that girl to the Virgins and Sluts thing tonight. I've heard of kids who visit their older siblings at college and go to parties and get totally wasted.

But Byron doesn't nibble. Not even close.

"Do you know your way out of here?" he asks.

"I think so," I say, slipping my feet into my shoes.

Byron hands me the Tupperware. "Thanks for the treats."

"You're welcome. I thought maybe it would…" I trail off.

"What?"

"Nothing."

Byron opens the door. "Look, Gin, the next time you want to come up here, can you give me a call first?"

I stare at my feet. "But I wanted to surprise you with the…" I hold up the container.

"Even so," Byron says.

As I head across campus, I feel a lump lodging in my throat. What I wanted to say a few minutes ago was *I thought maybe it would remind you how much you love me, how close we used to be.*

By the time I reach the subway station, tears are trickling down my cheeks. I keep wiping them away, but every time I do, more slide out to replace them.

When I arrive home, I have a headache. It feels like there's a thick band stretched around my forehead. I go into the kitchen and splash my face with water. Mom always leaves a few twenties on the counter in case I need anything. I dig through a drawer for a Chinese takeout menu, call up the restaurant, and order mu shu pork and fried veggie dumplings.

I head into my room and switch on the computer.

The More I Bare, The More I Scare
by Virginia Shreves

1. The Bri-girls would rather commit suicide than look like me.
2. No one ever believes Byron and I are related because he's cool and attractive and I'm, well, not.
3. If they filmed another Babe: Pig in the City, I'd get cast in the leading role.
4. If I eat a slice of pizza on the sidewalk, strangers give me nasty looks, like I'm supposed to live on lettuce until I've whittled down to the size of a chopstick.
5. Relatives don't send me clothes because they're scared to guess my size, so I have more gift boxes

of nail polish than the Revlon factory.

6. Whenever I picture myself squeezed into a black leather bustier and fishnets, I get violently ill.

7. If I were thin, maybe Byron would have invited me to the Virgins and Sluts party—or at least been happier to see me at his dorm.

By the time I've finished writing, my headache has subsided. I go online. I haven't heard from Shannon since Wednesday, so I'm starting to worry that the onion fumes are seriously depressing her. I exhale when I see her name in my inbox.

To: citigurl13
From: goddess_shannon
Date: Saturday, September 28, 4:29 p.m.
Subject: !!!!!

I'm running out the door, but I had to tell you that I think I'm making some real, live friends in Walla Walla! Stay tuned...

To: goddess_shannon
From: citigurl13
Date: Saturday, September 28, 4:53 p.m.
Subject: ?????

YOU CAN'T LEAVE ME HANGING LIKE THIS.

Who, what, when, where, and why?

* * *

As soon as I've sent the e-mail, I collapse on my bed. My forehead is tightening again. I must be an evil person, but I'm not exactly thrilled that Shannon is making new friends. What if she forgets about me? Besides, our bi-coastal boo-hoo-fest has offered me a certain degree of comfort, like I'm not alone in all my misery.

I roll over and stare out my window. I can see a narrow stretch of Riverside Park and the Hudson River. I've watched the most amazing sunsets from my bed, especially during late fall when the air is cool and clear.

The intercom rings. It must be the Chinese food. As I'm heading to the front door, it crosses my mind that if I don't go out tomorrow, the delivery guy is going to be the only human I'll see for the next twenty-four hours.

CHAPTER EIGHT

Froggy Welsh the Fourth has made it up my shirt!

Every star and planet must be perfectly aligned today. As Froggy and I rode the crosstown bus, we chatted more than usual. He described this graphic design competition that he's entering in a few weeks. We also discovered that we've both memorized the theme song to nearly every sitcom from the past decade.

As we walked toward my building, we knocked our hips against each other and sang a few verses from *Friends*.

The only glitch arose when we were in the elevator. As we got on in the lobby, we were joined by Mrs. Myers. She's an elderly woman who lives on the ninth floor. Whenever she goes to Miami to visit her grandnephew, I feed her Siamese cats.

As soon as we stepped into the elevator, I

noticed Mrs. Myers eyeing Froggy.

"Anaïs,"—she tapped her metal cane on my sneaker—"why don't you introduce me to your boyfriend?"

I wasn't sure whether to be more taken aback that Mrs. Myers confused me with my gorgeous sister or that she called Froggy my boyfriend.

"I'm Virginia."

"I *know* who you are." Mrs. Myers prodded her cane toward Froggy. "But who is *he*?"

"He's ... he's..." I desperately searched for a way to inform her that Froggy and I aren't boyfriend and girlfriend. "He's Froggy."

"*Froggy?*" Mrs. Myers looked puzzled.

The elevator arrived at the ninth floor. As she hobbled out, I heard her muttering, "What kind of name is *Froggy* for a handsome young boy?"

The door closed. I glanced fearfully at Froggy, but to my relief, he cracked up. I started laughing, too. By the time the elevator arrived at my apartment, we were both in hysterics.

We headed straight to my bedroom rather than stopping off for our usual snack. Froggy unlaced his sneakers and kicked them off. We flopped onto my bed and started making out. The kissing was intense from the start. Our lips were open. Our tongues took turns exploring the insides of each other's mouths. For a moment, I imagined myself as Meg Ryan in the last scene of *You've Got Mail*

when she finally learns that Tom Hanks is the man she loves. *That's* how good it felt.

When we finally came up for air, I planted a row of soft kisses along Froggy's earlobe. He moaned from deep in the back of his throat. The next thing I knew, his hands were inside my shirt.

I'd carefully selected my bra this morning. It's tan-colored, hardly as sexy as my black one, but easy to undo, with a simple hook in the back. Froggy got it on the first try. He eased my bra onto my collarbone, leaving my breasts bare under my shirt.

And now, for the first time in my life, a non-medical person is touching my chest. He's stroking my breasts, gently pulling at my nipples. It feels so good that I'm getting wet between my legs.

After a few minutes, Froggy rolls onto his back, so we're lying shoulder to shoulder. "Virginia?" he whispers.

"Yeah?"

"That felt good."

"I know."

"I've never done that before," Froggy says quietly.

"Me neither."

As Froggy caresses my hair, I snuggle into the crook of his neck. We're silent for a few minutes. I'm just thinking that this is the nicest moment in my entire life when I hear the front door unlock.

74

Froggy's body tenses up. We pull away from each other.

"Virginia?" Mom calls out. "Virginia?"

Froggy and I go into panic mode. We fly off my bed. I yank my bra around my boobs and hook it into place. As Mom knocks on my door, I gesture toward my bed.

Froggy flattens himself to the floor and slides awkwardly under the frame.

"Virginia?" Mom asks, turning my doorknob.

I thank my lucky stars that I always lock the door when Froggy's over.

"I'm here, Mom," I say.

My heart is racing. I make sure none of Froggy's appendages are exposed as I cross the room, attempt a calming breath, and open my door.

"Are you OK?" Mom asks. "Your face is flushed."

"I'm fine. I just fell asleep." I glance covertly at Froggy's backpack and trombone case. "Why are you home early?"

"Don't you remember? We have your doctor's appointment at four-thirty."

"What doctor's appointment?"

"I told you last week. That new doctor who specializes in adolescent medicine."

"I guess."

"Well, I'm glad you're home."

"Yeah," I say.

"I wanted to remind you that I'm planning to

discuss your weight with the new doctor." Mom pauses and adds, "Just so it doesn't come out of the blue."

I'm sure Froggy heard that.

I'm going to drop dead.

How could Froggy not have heard that?

I'm going to get a shovel, dig a huge hole in Central Park, and crawl into it. I'll pay someone to cover me up with dirt and put a stone on my grave that says: *Virginia Shreves, 15, died from utter humiliation.*

Mom looks like she's waiting for a response. Did she ask me a question?

"I guess," I say, shrugging my shoulders.

"Let's leave in ten minutes. I'll be in my study if you need me."

As soon as Mom is gone, I close the door.

"Coast clear?" Froggy whispers.

"I think so." I touch my flushed cheeks. It's all I can do to remember to breathe.

Froggy slides out from under my bed. As he brushes the dust balls off his clothes and laces up his sneakers, I can't look him in the eye.

We don't say a word to each other as we tiptoe through the apartment. I nudge him into the foyer. He waves goodbye, but I quietly close the front door.

I will never, ever, ever be able to face Froggy again.

* * *

I don't say anything for the entire cab ride up Broadway. The new doctor's office is near Columbia. That's almost forty blocks from our apartment, but Mom is on her cell phone the whole time, so she doesn't notice my silence.

As the cab pulls up to the corner nearest the hospital, Mom hangs up and turns to me. "Are you sure you're feeling OK?"

"Yeah."

"You still look flushed." Mom hands some cash up to the driver. "Maybe you should ask Dr. Love to take your temperature."

"Dr. Love?"

The driver gives Mom her change. She counts the bills and passes a tip to him. "Your new doctor."

I slide out of the cab. Someone named Dr. Love should sing lead vocals in a punk band. Or be a porn star. But my doctor? I picture some smarmy, fake-tanned doctor, the kind they cast in hospital soaps.

Fortunately, Dr. Love turns out to be nothing like I expected. He's young for a doctor, probably in his early thirties, with cappuccino-colored skin, dark eyelashes, and pencil-thin dreads poking out all over his head.

I'm sitting on the examining table when he walks in. Mom is out in the waiting room. I'm bemoaning the fact that the paper robe the nurse gave me is smaller than a cocktail napkin. I'm also wondering whether she groaned when she weighed me. It sounded like she did, but I never look at the scale, so I'm not sure whether it was bad news or *extremely* bad news.

Dr. Love sits on the revolving stool and extends his hand. "I'm Benjamin Love," he says. His voice is warm and soothing, like a bubble bath.

I shake his hand. "I'm Virginia."

We chat for a few minutes and then Dr. Love pulls out his stethoscope and wheels toward me. He listens to my lungs and heart, feels my nodes, and presses my appendix. Throughout the examination, he keeps murmuring "very healthy" and "excellent." When he takes a blood sample, he talks to me the whole time, so the needle barely hurts.

Once the exam is over, Dr. Love swivels around on his stool, writes something in my chart, and turns to face me again.

"When your mom made this appointment," he says, "she mentioned that she wanted the three of us to discuss your weight."

I stare at my bare feet dangling over the side of the examination table.

Dr. Love frowns. "This isn't something I usually like to do. You are my patient. I want you to feel you can be candid with me, that whatever you tell me won't get back to your mom." Dr. Love

 78

searches my face. "I'm only going to invite her in here if you're comfortable with it."

I tug at the robe. Why doesn't it cover more of my body? I should send an e-mail to the company that manufactures medical gowns and suggest they make them in a size other than extra-small.

"So?" Dr. Love asks.

I don't know what to say. I'm sure Mom is just trying to be helpful. But sometimes it feels like I'm beyond help, beyond hope.

"I guess it's OK," I say.

"You guess or you're sure?"

"I'm sure."

He stands up to leave. "I'll give you a few minutes to change back into your clothes."

"Thanks."

When they return, I'm sitting on the examination table, one knee over the other, my arms tight across my chest. Dr. Love settles onto his stool. Mom sits in the hard plastic chair.

Dr. Love rotates so he's facing Mom. "What did you want to discuss, Dr. Shreves?"

Mom's mouth twitches. "I'm concerned about Virginia's weight."

Dr. Love raises his eyebrows.

Mom continues. "I was heavy as a child, but I slimmed down by the time I was fifteen or sixteen. I've always assumed that's how it would be for Virginia, but it just doesn't seem to be happening."

I feel my cheeks flushing and my underarms are moist with sweat.

"May I ask why you've decided to address this now?" Dr. Love asks.

Mom fiddles with the clasp on her purse. She's much better at listening to other people's problems than discussing her own. "It's so hard being overweight. I want to do everything I can to make life easier for Virginia."

Dr. Love is quiet for a moment. When he finally speaks, he addresses me directly. "Let me start by saying that I prefer to look at things in terms of *health* instead of *weight*." He glances over at Mom, who shifts in her chair. "Until I get your blood work back, I can't give a comprehensive report on your health. But from the initial examination, you're very healthy, on par with most teenagers."

Dr. Love pauses before adding, "I want to be frank with you, however. While you're not in the range we classify as obese, you're heavier than average. If you continue to gain weight into adulthood, you'll be at risk for heart disease, hypertension, even diabetes. So while there's no reason to panic, it would be beneficial to start thinking about the long term."

I glance at Mom. She points her chin toward Dr. Love, as if to say, *Listen up*.

"I'd like you to re-evaluate your diet," he says.

"Cut down on carbs and greasy foods, exercise at least three times a week. Do you get much exercise?"

"I'm always encouraging Virginia to come to the gym with me," says Mom. "Exercise is how I keep my weight down, but she says she finds it boring."

Dr. Love frowns. "With all due respect, Dr. Shreves, I prefer not to focus on weight or body size. It's about fitness and nutrition and feeling good. Once those things fall into place, Virginia will become her natural body type"—Dr. Love gives Mom a long look—"which is different for every person."

Mom mashes her lips together.

"So?" Dr. Love asks.

"I'm not a jock, if that's what you're asking."

"You don't have to be a jock to get exercise." Dr. Love sets down my chart. "I'd be happy to help you figure this out, as long as you're up for the challenge. Is this what you want?"

Is this what I want? I want to not be embarrassed around Froggy. I don't want Brie to trash me behind my back. I don't want to get any more of those looks from Mom, like she feels sorry for me or she's ashamed of me. I want to be more like Anaïs and Byron. I want my parents to consider me Shreves-worthy.

Mom and Dr. Love are waiting for my response. I raise and lower my shoulders. "I want to be healthier."

For the next several minutes, Dr. Love talks about nutrition and nonjock ways to get a decent workout. I sit there, listening and nodding. Every once in a while, I glance over at Mom. I think I detect a tinge of pride on her face.

Mom drops me off on our corner and tells the cab-driver to continue to her office. As soon as I get upstairs, I won't allow myself to go into the kitchen, like I usually do. Instead, I check my e-mail. I haven't heard back from Shannon since Saturday, when I demanded the scoop on her friends. There's no word from Walla Walla, but there's a phone message from Dad.

"Ginny," he says on the voice-mail, "I've got two tickets to a Yankee playoff game on October nineteenth, assuming they make it that far, which you and I both know they will. Mom and I have a golf tournament in Connecticut that day, so I was thinking you and Byron might like to go."

A Yankee playoff game with my brother! I leave a breathless message with Byron, telling him to call me as soon as possible.

A few hours later, I'm hunched over the dining-room table, attempting to finish *The Scarlet Letter*. Dad walks into the room, munching a handful of cashews.

"Any word from Byron?"

I shake my head. "Not yet."

"I just got off the phone with Mom." Dad tosses back a few nuts. "Sounds like you had a productive appointment with that doctor."

"Yeah," I say, flipping to the next page in my book.

"It's a good thing." Dad picks a bit of cashew out of his teeth. "You've got a great face, Ginny. Think how much prettier you could be if you lost twenty or thirty pounds."

I feel like I've been punched in the stomach. I've always known that Dad was absent on the day they handed out tact. And I've always known that Dad is a fan of thin women. But he's never said it so bluntly—that I'm not that attractive the way I am.

I can't speak. I can't look up. If I do, I'll burst into tears.

If I lived in Nathaniel Hawthorne's time, I bet I'd have to wear a scarlet letter on my chest, just like Hester Prynne. Except in my case, it would be an "F" instead of an "A."

CHAPTER NINE

It's official. I'm on a diet.

In the four days since my appointment with Dr. Love, my entire life has changed. I can already fit two fingers into my normally snug waistband. Before long I'll be sticking an entire fist in there.

My goal is to lose as much as I can as quickly as possible. I'm not putting a number on it because I refuse to step on a scale unless I'm in a medical establishment. But all I know is that I want to get thin. And fast.

I've tried other diets before. Like in eighth grade when I decided to work out at Mom's gym. I stumbled along the treadmill every afternoon for a week. But after five days, I was bored to tears. I couldn't see the point in walking and walking and never getting anywhere. Or there was that time last year when Mom set up an appointment for me

 84

with Nan the Neurotic Nutritionist. Nan presented me with a food regimen that consisted of protein powders and low-carb bars. It made me parched just thinking about it. As soon as I left her office, I stopped by Häagen-Dazs and downed an entire dulce de leche milk shake just to get some moisture into my mouth.

But not this time. This time I'm taking it seriously.

All week long I didn't eat a real breakfast. I just grabbed a banana as I headed off to school. On Thursday I took a stalk of celery instead. *Big mistake.* I had to spend ten minutes in the bathroom at school extracting pale-green celery strings from my braces.

By lunchtime every day I was famished. Sometimes I even had a hunger headache. But rather than surrendering to my appetite, I'd close my eyes and play a Thin Virginia fantasy in my head. I'd visualize myself partying up at Columbia. *See how sexy I look in a bra and thong and hip-hugger jeans! How much will you charge ME to get into Virgins and Sluts?* I had tamer variations as well. Sometimes I'd be laughing with Byron as we jumped for foul balls at a Yankee game. Other times I'd suck in my stomach as Mom proudly introduced me to her colleagues at black-tie events. I even imagined Dad complimenting my body, like he used to with Anaïs. Except I wouldn't get angry at him and launch into a feminist tirade the way my sister did.

These visions were enough to make me skip lunch on Tuesday, Wednesday, Thursday, and Friday. I steered clear of the cafeteria to avoid being beckoned by Twinkies or a tray of tater tots. Also, it eliminated the stress of finding tablemates, which I couldn't handle on such a light head/empty stomach. Hiding out in the second-floor bathroom was out of the question, too. If I overheard another comment from the Bri-girls, I'd probably flush myself down a toilet.

My solution was to go to Ms. Crowley's office. She always welcomed me warmly. We'd chat for a few minutes, low-key stuff, like what I'm reading for "Ostracism and Oppression." Then she'd put me to work grading quizzes or suggesting Top 40 songs that could get kids excited about reading *The Grapes of Wrath*. Ms. Crowley is cool that way, trying to reach students on their level rather than just shoving dead authors down their throats all the time.

When she didn't have any work for me, I reviewed my notes from various classes. It was hard to concentrate during class all week, with my abdomen cramping and my brain pulsing from hunger. Sometimes I'd have to put my head on my desk for a few seconds and close my eyes. No one seemed to notice any difference in my behavior, though Ms. Crowley *did* observe that I was drinking a lot of water.

Diet Tip #1: Whenever you're hungry, chug a bottle of Poland Springs to fill your stomach.

I'm spending my days in a constant state of peeing or starvation. But I know this will all be worth it.

Besides, it's not like I have any alternative.

Friday night. My parents and I have a rare sit-down dinner. Dad cooks himself a steak, and Mom and I have salads and whole-wheat pita bread.

Diet Tip #2: Allow each bite to linger in your mouth for as long as humanly possible.

I slowly chew my plate of mixed greens and hungrily gaze at Dad's meat.

Dad catches my eye. "I have a proposition for you," he says.

"What?" I ask.

"How would you like me to take you on a shopping spree, to celebrate your new diet?"

Silence.

I glance at Mom. When Anaïs was in high school, Dad used to take her on sprees and they'd come home with great outfits. But my shopping always happens with Mom. She's good at picking out clothes with lots of strategic layers and camouflaging colors.

"Mike," Mom says, setting down her fork,

"maybe we should hold off on that for a while."

"I thought it would be fun for Ginny," Dad says. "A reward."

Mom looks at me. I shrug, as if to say, *Don't ask me … I just work here.*

"It would be wonderful to take Virginia shopping once she's slimmed down," Mom says. "But if she buys things now, they'll probably be a few sizes too big before long. I think we should wait until she reaches some kind of weight goal. Besides, it can be incentive for her to keep it up. Then it'll be a *real* reward."

"Do you have a weight goal?" Dad asks.

I shake my head.

Dad carves off a generous bite of steak. "Maybe you should make one."

"I don't do scales," I mumble, thinking how Dr. Love said he doesn't like to focus on weight.

Mom cuts in. "Why don't we call it a 'body goal' instead?"

Dad raises his wineglass. "Once you've reached your body goal, we'll hit the stores."

"Great," says Mom. "It's all set."

Mom and Dad look over at me. Did I even want to go on a shopping spree? Do I have a body goal? Sometimes my parents are so sure of what's best for me that I don't stop to think about what I really want.

I push aside my plate of lettuce.

*　　*　　*

Saturday morning. I'm sitting on my bedroom floor, flipping through *Fitness*. All week long I've been sifting through magazines, scouring them for diet tips. Whenever I find a valuable one, I clip it out and add it to a pile on my dresser. Mom and Dad are in Connecticut, so I'm blasting the radio and humming along.

I turn the page and stare down at a picture of a waify young model. Her upper arms have the circumference of my pinky. I tear out the page. Then I thumb through the rest of the magazine, ripping out the skinniest girls, the ones I'm most aiming to resemble.

These models will be my Food Police. They'll be my thinspiration. They'll help me reach my body goal.

I carry the magazine scraps to the kitchen and stick them to the refrigerator door with magnets.

For the rest of the day, whenever I reach into the fridge for a hunk of Cheddar cheese or some frozen cookie dough, I'll catch sight of the Food Police.

Don't do it, they'll say. *Not if you want to be thin like us.*

So I'll chug a gallon of water and find something more low-fat to do.

Sunday morning. My parents return from Connecticut early because Dad has to leave for a business trip to Chicago this afternoon. I'm sitting on the couch, watching TV and chewing my fat-free nails. They say hi to me and then Mom goes into the kitchen to make a smoothie.

A moment later she appears in the living room again.

"Virginia, I'm so proud of you," she says.

I mute the volume. It's not every day I hear "Virginia" and "proud" in the same sentence.

"Why?"

"I just saw those pictures you stuck on the fridge."

Mom, meet the Food Police.

Mom continues. "You want to hear something funny?"

I nod.

"Back when I was ..."—Mom pauses—"... a teenager. I put images of models on *my* family's fridge, to keep me from eating too much."

"Really?"

Mom nods. "Like mother, like daughter."

As she heads back into the kitchen, I pump the volume on the TV again.

Since when did Mom become Ms. Observant Parent? A few weeks ago, I got an A+ on a language arts paper about *One Hundred Years of Solitude* by Gabriel García Márquez. I even managed to include two mentions of "ostracism" and three of "oppression," so my teacher gobbled it up.

I stuck it to the fridge with a few magnets, hoping Mom—a big Márquez fan—would say something, but she never seemed to notice.

So how is it that she's in the apartment seven minutes and already spots the Food Police?

Oh well. I should probably look on the bright side of things.

Mom has never said *like mother, like daughter* to me before.

And that in itself is worth one hundred years of hunger.

Sunday afternoon. Mom is taking a step-aerobics class at her gym. Dad is picking up some toiletries so he can pack for Chicago. I'm stretched on the couch, painting my nails and reviewing some chemistry notes.

Diet Tip #3: If you feel the need to feed, grab some polish; by the time your nails have dried, the craving will have subsided.

The front door unlocks. Dad comes in, toting several plastic bags.

I'm about to greet him when I notice he's not alone. Two brutish men are hauling an oblong object wrapped in brown paper into our apartment. They set it down in the hallway. Dad hands them some money.

"What's that?" I call out as soon as they're gone.

"It's yours!" Dad exclaims.

"Mine? What is it?"

"Come in here and find out for yourself."

Once I'm in the hallway, Dad says, "Open it up."

I stare at the object. I'm usually a sucker for presents, but I have a funny feeling about this one. As I sit on the ground and tear away the brown paper, my heart sinks.

It's a mirror. A tell-all, show-all, full-length mirror.

"What do you think?" Dad is hovering expectantly above me.

"It's a mirror," I say glumly.

"I noticed you didn't have a mirror in your bedroom," Dad says. "I thought if you could watch yourself losing weight, it might help you reach your body goal."

Since when did Dad become Mr. Observant Parent? This past spring my computer was constantly crashing, shutting down in the middle of tasks, losing homework files. Whenever I asked Dad to help me with it, he always said things like, *I'm so busy … I'll look at it this weekend… Sorry, I'll check it out next week.* I finally got Shannon's mom, a computer whiz, to come over and straighten it out.

So how is it that he suddenly has time to take a complete inventory of my bedroom *and* fill in all the gaps?

Dad glances at his watch. "I'd better start packing for my flight. Will you help me carry this into your room?"

I remain on the floor, staring at the mirror.

Dad wraps his arms around the mirror and grunts as he lifts it by himself. "Come on, Ginny, give me a hand."

I've barely eaten anything today, so my head feels light. I slowly stand up and help him carry the mirror into my room.

Later Sunday afternoon. Dad is on his way to the airport. Mom just called from the gym to say she's staying longer to do weights. I'm slumped on the couch watching a *Friends* rerun. Whenever I've seen *Friends* these past few days, I've gotten a pang inside as I remember how Froggy and I sang the theme song together last Monday.

Ever since last week, I've been too humiliated to look him in the eye. I mean, he knows I saw a doctor about my weight. What could be more embarrassing than that?

Froggy and I are only in French class together, so it hasn't been hard to avoid him. Whenever I see him in the halls, I pretend to be fascinated by the cover of my notebook or an imaginary insect whizzing through the air. I've steered clear of the cafeteria and the computer cluster. And we sit two rows apart in French, so I'm careful not to glance in his direction. I still haven't figured out what I'll do tomorrow, when we usually have our Monday tryst at my apartment.

Once *Friends* is over, I switch off the TV with the remote control. I'm dying to check my e-mail. I haven't heard from Shannon in eight days. Last night I called her in Walla Walla, but her voice sounded weird as she rushed me off the phone, promising I'd be hearing from her soon.

As soon as I stand up, my head feels fuzzy, like I'm blacking out. My energy is so low. I collapse back onto the couch, sink my head between my knees, and take several deep breaths. After a few minutes I rise again, but slower this time.

I promised myself I'd only stay in my bedroom long enough to do e-mail. But after I log on—still no word from Shannon—I can't stop glancing at the mirror leaning against the wall between my desk and bookshelf.

I go over to my dresser, scoop up the pile of diet tips I've been collecting, and wedge them into the mirror's frame. That way, whenever I glimpse my reflection, at least I'll be comforted by the fact that I'm doing something about it.

I take a few steps backward to admire my work. That's when I catch sight of myself. I'm wearing baggy sweats and an oversize T-shirt, so it's hard to get a good reading on my body. I have to admit I'm curious to see how six days of starvation has

 94

left me. I know I'm not about to appear on the cover of *Maxim*, but maybe I'll have a little bit of a waist or something.

I sit on the edge on my bed and pull down my sweats. I yank my shirt over my head. I pause before unhooking my bra and wriggling out of my undies, but if I'm going to do this, I'm going to go full throttle.

As I walk toward the center of my room, my heart is thumping against my chest. I *never, ever, ever* look at myself in the mirror naked. When I get into the shower, I always turn the other way as I'm passing the mirror. Obviously I've seen myself as I'm lathering up or getting undressed, but that's different. That's just a little skin here and there. Not the complete and honest picture.

I take a few shallow breaths before reaching the mirror. This probably isn't the best idea. Not yet, anyway. But there's some force pulling me to the mirror, the same kind that makes me finish a jumbo bag of M&M's when I know I should stop after a few handfuls.

One more step and…

Oh no.

This is why Mom dragged me to Dr. Love.

This is why Dad bought me a full-length mirror.

This is why Brie would rather kill herself than be me.

This is why Froggy won't be seen with me in public.

As I stare at my naked body, I remember an article I once read about a sorority in California. The girls all had to strip down and stand in a line. Then the sorority president went down the row with a big black marker. As she stopped at each girl, she circled onto her skin wherever she needed to lose weight or tone up.

I direct my eyes to my stomach. This'll be the first to go. I grab a fold of my tummy and squeeze. It hurts, but a good pain, like I'm showing my body who's boss. I squeeze it once more, so hard that I suck in my breath.

Next, I zero in on my outer thighs. They're dimpled with cellulite, resembling a tub of cottage cheese. I pinch the flesh on my thighs between my fingers and thumb.

I rotate around and check out my butt.

What's the opposite of buns of steel? Buns of dough. Buns of butter.

I pinch and squeeze all over my butt cheeks, so hard that it leaves red marks. I'm choking back tears, but I keep telling myself that I deserve this. I got myself this way.

I proceed to pinch every unsightly part of my body—my inner thighs, my upper arms, my breasts, my hips. It happens in a colorless blur, like a pinwheel spinning too fast. I'm pinching and crying, crying and pinching. Snot is running down my nose and dripping saltily into my mouth, but I

96

keep grabbing at my skin, harder every time.

I sink onto the floor and curl up into the fetal position. I sob and shake and hug my knees and suck my knuckles.

Sometimes I wish I could just disappear from this earth, float away, like an old plastic bag that gets caught in a gust and carried over the Manhattan skyline.

CHAPTER TEN

It's a drizzly, cold Monday morning. The spots where I pinched myself are now eggplant-colored bruises. Most are located on regions of my body that are easy to conceal, but the big trick today is to avoid gym. I always change in a bathroom stall, so the locker room isn't a problem. But flouncing around in shorts and a T-shirt definitely puts me at high risk for bruise exposure—especially the ones on my thighs and upper arms.

It won't break my heart to skip gym. We've just started a unit called "Shoots and Ladders." Typical gym-teacher glorification of tumbling on mats, climbing ropes, and hanging precariously from clammy rings. I hate it. I loathe it. I detest, despise, and abhor it. There aren't enough words to express how much I dislike clutching a gnarled rope as our pint-sized instructor, also known as Teri the Tiny

 98

Gym Teacher, barks "Come on, Shreves! At least give it a try!" If it's not bad enough that there's no way in hell I have the upper-body strength to lift myself from the ground, factor in Brie Newhart, Brinna Livingston, and Briar Schwartz perpetually smirking at me from the mats.

As the second-period bell rings, summoning me to gym, I head to Paul the School Nurse's office. Paul the School Nurse is my secret weapon at Brewster. He's monumentally trying to over-compensate for his male-nurse status. Utter a syllable about cramps or PMS and he's bemoaning the woes of womanhood, feeling your menstrual pain.

Along with ditching gym, I also have to dodge Froggy. Even if he hadn't overheard that weight comment, there's no way I could fool around with him today. Let's say he lifted up my shirt and saw the welts on my stomach and hips. That would be a fun one to explain. *Oh, didn't I tell you? In my spare time, I like to pinch myself.*

We usually meet on the front steps of school and walk to the crosstown bus together. I've decided that I'm simply not going to show up. It's not like we've ever made a verbal agreement to both be there, so what's keeping me from being otherwise occupied? I know I should probably tell him, but I'm too chicken for that. Like, what if he asks for an explanation? *Because you know*

I'm seeing a Fat Doctor. Because I'm covered in bruises. Or worse, what if he says something like, *Why are you telling me this? I thought we were just going to keep it casual. I hope you're not starting to think we're boyfriend and girlfriend or anything.*

No, no, no. That would put me at risk of breaking the Fat Girl Code of Conduct, rule #4. Never make him discuss your relationship. Better to avoid the situation altogether.

My last class of the day is math. Mr. Moony's heart must be acting up because he's panting like a golden retriever as he hands out worksheets on the Pythagorean theorem. I attempt to concentrate on $a^2 + b^2 = c^2$, but I'm growing increasingly anxious about a potential Froggy encounter.

The bell rings. Rather than heading down the front stairwell with the other kids, I slink down a rear flight to the second floor and peek into Ms. Crowley's office. She's working at her computer, so I slip inside, remove the stack of books from her extra chair, and sit down. Ms. Crowley holds up a finger to signal that she'll be with me soon.

After a moment she says, "How's it going?"

"OK, I guess."

"Is everything all right?"

"What do you mean?"

"You seem a little distracted recently. Your eyes don't have their usual sparkle."

 100

"I'm fine," I say. "I'm just trying to lose some weight."

Ms. Crowley frowns. "Is a doctor helping you?"

"Sort of."

Ms. Crowley pulls a rubber band out of her hair and rolls it over her wrist. "I think it's great that you want to take control of your weight and I hope you're doing it in a healthy manner, but I have to warn you that dieting is a slippery slope."

I pick up a paper clip from her desk. "A slippery slope?"

"I know how difficult it is to be a large woman in this society," Ms. Crowley says. "Do you think I don't know that students call me Ms. *Cow*ley behind my back?"

I wonder if Ms. Crowley overheard them the way I overheard the Bri-girls in the bathroom that day. I wonder if it made her gnaw on her cheeks until they were raw.

"I've heard everything," Ms. Crowley says. "You name it, I've been called it. When I was younger, it affected me so strongly that I had some close calls with crash dieting, one where I spent a week in the hospital with a tube in my arm, feeding me nutrients."

"Are you serious?" I unbend the paper clip until it's a straight line.

"I was in my early twenties. I'm not telling you this to scare you. I'm just asking you to be careful.

101

Don't try to change everything overnight."

I jab the paper clip wire into the palm of my hand, not hard enough to break skin, but enough to leave tiny indentations. I understand what Ms. Crowley is saying. But that doesn't take away Workout Fiend Mom and Naturally Thin Dad and Beautiful Anaïs and Built-Like-A-Greek-God Byron.

I stayed in Ms. Crowley's office long enough to avoid Froggy after school on Monday. But that means I have to face him in French this morning. As I head down the language corridor, I hug my books to my chest.

There are a million reasons why I hate French. First of all, I suck at it, which is so frustrating because it totally pulls down my otherwise straight-A grade point average. I can spend an entire evening memorizing irregular verbs, but when I wake up the next morning, it's like they've leaked out of my brain and onto my pillow.

I really wanted to take Chinese. I thought it would be fun to be able to tell people off in Chinese. Unless you're in Chinatown, no one will know what you're saying. But Mom insisted that I have to take French because every other Shreves converses fluently in it. She says I can only take Chinese after I've finished my three-year language requirement.

I also hate French because my teacher is evil. Mademoiselle Kiefer—born and bred in Erie, Pennsylvania, but a total French wannabe—wears black all the time and has long spidery legs. I've nicknamed them the baguette legs because it looks like her torso is propped atop two narrow loaves of French bread. Mademoiselle Kiefer is certifiably bipolar, except her pole lands on the Arctic side of things 99.9 percent of the time. She's always swearing at us in French. The only people she's nice to are the popular kids. There are several in my class, including Brie Newhart and Brinna Livingston. Brie is her pet, probably because she's named after a French cheese. Last week she let Brie go into the hallway to make a call even though cell phones are banned during school hours.

When I arrive in class, most kids are already seated. Brie and Brinna are milling around Mademoiselle Kiefer's desk, comparing notes on their favorite Left Bank bistros. Brie twirls her sandy curls into a French twist and says how she knows Paris like the back of her hand. Brinna murmurs and nods. I don't think Brinna's family are as wealthy as Brie's, but she's always acting like they are.

As I slide into my seat, I force myself not to look in Froggy's direction.

The bell rings.

Brie and Brinna head to their desks. Brie's high-heeled Parisian boots click down the aisle as she takes her seat, one row to my left. I make a special attempt to turn my eyes away from Brie, but I have to admit it's hard. She flirted with my brother on the subway, for god's sake! She now knows exactly who I am. So how can she still sit three feet from me and act like I'm a nonperson?

Mademoiselle Kiefer slams a hole-punch onto her desk to get everyone's attention. "*Bienvenue*," she barks, welcoming everyone to class.

Mademoiselle Kiefer writes *Weather Expressions* on the chalkboard. I copy it into my notebook. Then she rattles off various ways to describe the elements. Oddly, she only seems to be teaching us foul-weather phrases such as "It's cold" and "It's windy."

I feel a sharp jab in my arm. I glance to my left. I'm shocked to see Brie holding a folded piece of paper with my name on it. As I grab it, I attempt to offer her a smile of thanks, but she won't make eye contact with me. Oh yeah, I might contaminate her perfectly popular reputation. Or maybe she thinks my cellulite is contagious.

It's an expertly folded note, with five different edges poking into various flaps. I carefully unfold it. The first thing I notice is Froggy's handwriting. He writes with scrupulous block letters—very neat, very consistent.

104

VIRGINIA—
WHERE WERE YOU YESTERDAY?
I WAITED ON THE STOOP FOR FORTY-FIVE MINUTES.
IS EVERYTHING OK?
☹
FROGGY WELSH THE QUATRIÈME

I am shocked.

I am stunned.

Froggy knows I'm going to a Fat Doctor and he still wants to fool around!

I'm about to climb on top of my desk and whoop for joy when it hits me that I actually have to answer Froggy's question about why I stood him up.

I chew my lower lip for a second. A white lie will have to do.

F—
I was feeling sick so I went home early.
Sorry.
V

I refold the paper, cross out my name, and print *Froggy* on the outside.

Ordinarily I wouldn't ask anything of Brie.

Iron Rule of the High School Way of Life: Only address a popular kid if they address you first. Don't just approach them and strike up a conversation, unless it's a matter of life and death—and even then, it should be a matter of the popular person's life or death.

This isn't life and death, but it's pretty important.

I work up my nerve before lightly tapping Brie's bony forearm.

I can see her flinch, but she pretends to be enraptured by Mademoiselle Kiefer's lecture on crappy weather.

I poke Brie again.

"Hmph!" she snorts.

Mademoiselle Kiefer spins around and glares at me. I cower like an abused puppy. As soon as she turns back to the board, Brie snatches the note out of my hands and tosses it at Froggy's feet.

"*Il fait mauvais* means it's stormy," Mademoiselle Kiefer says. "*Il pleut.* That's what you say when it's raining."

I can see Froggy writing on a fresh page, tearing it from his spiral notebook, and folding it up.

Brie flings a new note onto the floor near my desk. I slide out of my chair and swipe up the paper.

VIRGINIA—
MAYBE WE SHOULD TAKE A TRIP TO WALLA WALLA TOGETHER.
WOULD THAT MAKE YOU FEEL BETTER?
☺
FW4

I'm puzzled.

I've never talked to Froggy about Shannon, so how does he know about Walla Walla? And why a vacation there?

I turn to Froggy, scrunch my eyebrows together, and mouth, *Walla Walla?*

Froggy pantomimes a swimming/crawling gesture and tugs at his sweatshirt. At that same moment, someone's cell phone starts playing an instrumental version of the French national anthem. Mademoiselle Kiefer spins around in time to catch Froggy while he's still in action.

"That's it, *ma petite grenouille*," she snarls. "Into the hallway."

I can see Brie quietly tucking a small pink cell phone into her bag. An uncomfortable laughter ripples through the classroom. Mademoiselle Kiefer has just called Froggy her "little frog." I only know that because I recently looked up "frog" in my French-English dictionary.

"*Excusez-moi?*" Froggy asks as he rubs his nose. He's definitely not the type of kid who's ever sent into the hallway. He's plays *trombone,* after all.

Mademoiselle Kiefer angrily extends her arm in the direction of the hallway, as if to say: *Don't doubt the magnitude of my evil.*

Froggy gathers together his folders. As he stands up, he turns to me and yanks his sweatshirt

107

one more time.

"*Maintenant!*" growls Mademoiselle Kiefer.

Once Froggy is in the hallway, I turn it over and over in my head. *Crawling. Tugging at sweatshirt. Swimming. Crawling.* That's it! When Froggy crawled under my bed last week, he must have seen my WALLA WALLA IS FOR LOVERS sweatshirt that I kicked under there a few weeks ago. I'd almost forgotten about that sweatshirt from Shannon. I smile as I ponder the romantic implications of Froggy suggesting we go to Walla Walla together. Walla Walla is for *lovers*, after all.

Mademoiselle Kiefer stomps toward me.

"Is there some joke you want to share with the rest of us, La Vierge?"

The class cracks up. I can hear Brie's high, hiccupy laugh above everyone else's.

"No," I say.

Mademoiselle Kiefer marches back to the board. I flip through my French-English dictionary. When I come to *vierge*, I feel my cheeks heating up. I have just been called "The Virgin" in front of the entire class. If there's ever a self-prophesying name, mine's the one. At least *la grenouille* was out of earshot.

(HAPTER ELEVEN

To: citigurl13
From: goddess_shannon
Date: Wednesday, October 9, 5:38 p.m.
Subject: H.A. is not funny

Virginia—

I'm soooooo sorry for my absence. I hope you're not mad at me. I've been on House Arrest. For the past ten days, Liam and Nina have not allowed me to talk on the phone, watch TV, or do e-mail. Death by denial of technology.

It's all because of my new friends. There are three of them— two guys, Evan and Hunter, and a girl named Sabrina. Most people at Walla Walla High School think they're freaks. Hunter has aquamarine hair and Sabrina has "Mom" tattooed on her arm. But I don't care. They were the only people who treated me like something other than a stuttering misfit.

Last Saturday night, the four of us decided to meet at a

playground near my house. It was just going to be some after-dinner hanging out, but we started talking and walking and talking and talking. GUESS WHAT? I didn't stutter around them, not even once.

The next thing I knew it was one-thirty. IN THE MORNING.

I sprinted all the way home, but when I got there, Liam and Nina were hysterical. They thought I'd been squished by farm machinery. They yelled at me. I called them "onion-loving fuckers" and locked myself in the bathroom. That's when I was slapped with H.A. Liam and Nina say they're happy I'm making friends, but that still doesn't mean I can stay out all night. Whatever.

Love,
Shannon

P.S. Sabrina, Evan, Hunter, and I have been sitting together at lunch all week. Evan eats cubes of tofu doused in peanut sauce.

To: goddess_shannon
From: citigurl13
Date: Wednesday, October 9, 5:47 p.m.
Subject: H.A. is DEFINITELY not funny

Shan—
Good to hear from you. I was about to file a Missing Persons report. I'm not mad, but I wish you'd found a way to tell me what was up, like snail mail.

 110

Congrats on your new friends. They sound interesting. Are you sure Sabrina's tattoo is real?

Shan, may I admit something? I'm a little worried that you're going to forget your boring old best friend now that you've found these exciting new people. Well, I hope you know that I won't let you escape that easily.

Even if I have to start eating tofu.

Love,
Gin

P.S. Speaking of eating, have I told you I'm on a diet? For real this time.
P.P.S. Things on the Froggy front are starting to improve.
P.P.P.S. Just thought I'd remind you that you never stutter around me either.

I'm sitting on my bed, struggling to conjugate verbs in the *passé composé*. Mademoiselle Kiefer gave us a worksheet of verbs that we have to transform into the past tense. I've heard that in Chinese you don't have to make verb forms change for tenses. What a far superior language.

There's a knock on my door.

"Come in," I shout.

Mom peeks into my room. "How was school?"

"Fine."

"Anything interesting happen?"

"Not really."

111

"Would you like to go out to dinner?"

I drop my pencil. "Just you and me?"

Mom nods.

I can't remember the last time Mom and I went to a restaurant, just the two of us. She's always so busy with her patients and her exercise and everything. Besides, she usually has dinner with Nan the Neurotic Nutritionist on Wednesday nights.

"What about Nan?"

"Nan's out of town," Mom says, "so I thought it would be nice to have a little mother-daughter time."

Mom gives Dad a quick call in Chicago and then we walk down to Citrus, this elegant Mexicany-Japanesey restaurant on Amsterdam Avenue. It's a mild fall night, the last gasps of summer. The sidewalks are buzzing with people and strollers and dogs straining at their leashes. With each step, I squeeze my butt cheeks together.

Diet Tip #4: Find creative ways to exercise undesirable body parts.

Mom orders a glass of chardonnay. I get a Diet Sprite. When the waiter brings our drinks, he plops a basket of multicolored tortilla chips and a bowl of salsa onto the table. I'm zooming in for a chip when I catch Mom's eye.

Diet Tip #5: Utilize something other than a grease-drenched chip to eat salsa.

I scoop up some salsa with my spoon. Mom smiles approvingly.

 112

As I drink my Sprite through a straw, Mom starts talking about her patients. She never calls them by name, so she won't break their confidentiality. It's more like the Girl Who Swallows Pocket Change When She's Upset or the Boy Who Shoplifts Even Though His Parents Are Millionaires. Mom's stories often shock me. I can't believe how screwed up some people are.

I'm tempted to tell Mom about Shannon's e-mail. I'm curious to see if she thinks I'm in danger of being replaced by the Walla Walla friends. But I decide not to mention anything. After listening to problems all day, Mom's tolerance for hearing mine is usually pretty low. Sometimes at night, as she's making a mug of tea or curling up with a novel, she'll sigh and say, *I'm glad my children have turned out so healthy*. Having a stable family is important to Mom, probably because her own childhood was so rocky.

I spoon up some more salsa and study the menu. Whenever we've been to Citrus before, I've gotten the cheesy fajita platter. But this time around, I'm determined to order something light, like sushi. Maybe that will score me another approving maternal smile.

CHAPTER TWELVE

Shannon hasn't been the only Missing Person. I haven't spoken with Byron since the day I brought him the Rice Krispie treats. I've left him three voice-mail messages and even sent a few e-mails asking about that Yankee game to which Dad is offering us tickets. New York beat Oakland in the Division Series, so if they can hang on in the play-offs, it looks like this game will happen. It's a big-deal game to any Yankee fan, especially one who aspires to bear the offspring of several players.

Unfortunately, no one's heard a peep from Byron, not even my parents.

That's what Dad and I are arguing about now. It's Thursday evening. Mom is doing her group-therapy night. Dad has just returned from his business trip. He's reclining on the ottoman and watching the news. I'm sitting on the floor, removing my nail polish with a cotton ball. This afternoon, while in the throes of munchie-mania, I painted each finger a different color. After applying Strobe, Zippy, Sizzle, Tidal Wave, and Firecracker, I decided the rainbow thing was too flashy for someone like me.

Every time there's a commercial, Dad and I start arguing again.

"If Byron can't give you definite word by tonight," Dad says, "I'll have to give the tickets to one of my colleagues."

"Dad, you can't! It's a playoff game and you said I could go." I attempt to throw a cotton ball at him, but it lands an inch in front of me.

"I'm afraid I have no other choice, Ginny. The game is next Saturday, so I've got to get something figured out. Mom and I will be in Connecticut all weekend, and I can't let you go to Yankee Stadium alone."

I unscrew a bottle of mauve and polish my middle finger. "Who says I'd go alone?"

"Is there another person you had in mind?"

Sometimes Dad can be as sensitive as a cement block. I search my brain for an answer. Normally I would say Shannon and that would be that. Who can I bring now? Froggy? We've actually been talking in school a little more recently. Like in French class today, he asked to be my partner for Everyday Conversation. That's what Mademoiselle

Kiefer has us do whenever she wants to go chase after the sexy male physics teacher. But I'm not about to ask Froggy on a date. That's in total violation of the Fat Girl Code of Conduct, rule #1. No riding the moped in public. Besides, Froggy is a Red Sox fan. He has a bunch of their stickers plastered on his trombone case.

The news comes on. Dad pumps the volume. I've just finished my left hand when the phone rings.

"Would you get that?" Dad asks.

As I stomp into the hallway, I suspend my hand in the air so I won't smudge my nails. My only hope at this point is that it's Byron, finally calling back to say he can come to the game.

I pick up the cordless phone. "Hello?"

"I'm calling for Dr. or Mr. Shreves," a man says. His voice sounds deep and official.

"May I ask who's calling?"

"This is Maxwell Briggs." He pauses before adding, "The dean of students at Columbia University."

"Hold on please."

I cover the mouthpiece as I carry the phone into the living room and tap Dad's shoulder.

"It's for you," I whisper. "Sounds important."

Dad mutes the volume on the TV, clears his throat, and lifts the phone to his ear. "This is Mike Shreves," he says.

116

I flounce onto the couch and blow at my finger-tips. I'm half watching the news and half listening to Dad's side of the conversation. He's not saying much, just an occasional "I see" and "of course."

My ears only perk up when I hear Dad ask, "Are you sure there hasn't been a mistake, sir?"

I don't think I've heard Dad use the word "sir" since a doctor called from a Phoenix hospital three years ago to report that his father had had a stroke.

"What was that about?" I ask as Dad switches off the phone.

Dad is staring blankly at the television. The color has leaked from his face, leaving him a sickly greenish hue. The last time Dad looked this bad was the day he got the phone call about Grandpa Shreves.

I don't know how much time has passed.

I'm sitting on my bed. I've just devoured an entire box of Frosted Flakes, handful by handful. I hear my parents' voices rising and falling in the living room. Mom's voice is high and squeaky. Dad's sounds drained, devoid of emotion.

The phone rings. I hear Mom scamper to get it. I hear shrill sobs. I hear someone go to the liquor cabinet and pour a drink.

I concentrate on numbing myself. That's what I've been doing ever since the phone call from Dean Briggs. I've started with my heart and am expanding outward to the rest of my body. Now I am numbing my arms and legs, elbows and knees.

There's a knock on my door.

I don't answer.

Another knock.

I don't answer.

The door cracks open, so I stuff the empty cereal box under my covers.

I turn to face Mom. There are smears of mascara under her red-rimmed eyes.

When she speaks, her voice sounds like a deflated balloon. "I assume you've heard."

I nod.

Mom opens her mouth. This is the point in the conversation where she generally lapses into ShrinkSpeak, offering a Dr. Phyllis Shreves therapized explanation. But nothing comes out.

We stare at each other for several seconds.

Mom wipes under her eyes with the side of her finger. "Byron is moving home tomorrow."

I continue staring at her.

"He'll be living here until we can get this straightened out."

I turn to the window.

"There must be some mistake," Mom says. "I've known Byron for his entire life. I know who he is and how his brain operates and what he's capable of. And my son is certainly not capable of something like this. *That* I can guarantee."

 118

There's a red light flashing in New Jersey.

"What's wrong, Virginia? Why aren't you saying anything?"

I concentrate on numbing my ankles and wrists.

"How do you feel about this?"

Now my hands and feet. Now my fingers and toes.

Mom switches off my light as she leaves my room.

citigurl13: It's 1:12 a.m. in NYC and I can't sleep. Are you online? If not, I'm going to keep instant-messaging you all night.

goddess_shannon: I'm online! I was about to e-mail you that you'll ALWAYS be my spiritual twin no matter what … Hold on! What's up? Is everything OK?

citigurl13: No. But I'm still in shock. I can't talk about it.

goddess_shannon: Talk.

citigurl13: It's too horrendous.

goddess_shannon: Talk.

citigurl13: Consider yourself warned.

goddess_shannon: Warned.

citigurl13: Byron was found guilty of date-raping a girl at Columbia.

goddess_shannon: Holy shit.

citigurl13: He's suspended for the rest of the semester. He's moving home tomorrow.

goddess_shannon: Do you know who she is? Do you know when it happened?

citigurl13: All I know is that it has something to do with this Virgins and Sluts party he went to a few weeks ago.

goddess_shannon: Now I'M in shock. Date rape?

citigurl13: I know. I can hardly breathe. I have a huge lump in my throat. I just ate half a box of Ritz crackers. Do you know how many calories that is?

goddess_shannon: Screw your diet. Are you going to be OK?

citigurl13: I'll either be OK or I'll drink a bottle of Clorox.

goddess_shannon: Please tell me you're not serious.

citigurl13: I'm not serious.

citigurl13: For the most part, anyway.

CHAPTER THIRTEEN

I barely sleep all night. Every time I roll over, I grind against a Frosted Flake. But I don't feel them. I don't feel anything. I'm working extremely hard at being numb.

I'm going to stay home sick today. I hardly have the energy to sleep, much less take a shower, get dressed, and deal with school.

The phone rings around 6:45 A.M. It doesn't sound like anyone is answering it, so I pick up my line. I'm surprised to hear Shannon's voice on the other end, stuttering up a storm. For some reason, Mom always makes her nervous.

"I'm c-c-c-calling for Virg-g-g-inia."

"I'm not sure she's awake yet," Mom says.

I cut in. "I've got it, Mom."

"I'm so sorry for c-c-c-calling this early, Ms. Shreves. I mean, Doc-Doc-Doc-Doc—"

"That's all right."

"Virginia!" Shannon shouts as soon as Mom hangs up. "I set my alarm for the middle of the night, Walla Walla time, so I could catch you before you left for school."

"I'm not going to school today, but I'm glad you called." It's great to hear Shannon's voice. It's been awhile since we've had a real conversation. Shannon prefers e-mail because telephones make her stutter more.

"I wanted to make sure you didn't swallow any Clorox. I was worried."

"I'm still alive," I say. "Unfortunately."

Shannon ignores my comment. "Why aren't you going to school?"

"I just don't want to deal with it."

"Not to sound preachy, but you should go. Do you really want to be there when Byron moves in?"

I hadn't thought of that. I'm definitely not ready to see him yet, to acknowledge that this whole thing is happening. "I guess not."

"Well, hurry along then."

"OK, Mommy." I wedge the phone between my ear and shoulder as I cross the room to my dresser.

"Before you go, may I read you something?"

"What?" I ask. As I root around in my top drawer for a pair of undies, my hand brushes against my cedar chest, the one where I keep my treasured possessions.

 122

"I came across this quote on a box of Sleepytime tea last night," says Shannon. "Someone named John Muir. I think he saved forests."

I sit on the edge of my bed.

"Here goes: 'When we try to pick out anything by itself, we find it hitched to everything else in the universe.'" Shannon pauses before adding, "I think it means that everything's connected. Or maybe that no single incident stands by itself."

"Are you saying you think Byron has done this to other girls?" I ask, twisting the phone cord around my index finger. I can tell my voice sounds sharp, but this is my big brother we're talking about, my hero, the person with whom I always wished I could be orphaned. I'm not ready to start thinking about him as a serial rapist.

"No," Shannon says quickly. "I just thought of you when I read it ... but maybe I was a little dopey from the tea."

"I don't know," I say.

"Neither do I."

I can't believe I make it to school. I'm in a total daze. All I want to do is crawl into my locker and fall asleep.

My first class is global studies II. It should be called murder studies II. Last year in global studies I, we learned about every mass slaughter in history—from the Native Americans to the

123

Holocaust. This year we're focusing on contemporary world issues. We have to read the *New York Times* and surf CNN.com at least once a week. I thought it would be more upbeat than last year, but Mr. Vandenhausler has once again focused on death and destruction. We've just finished learning about the genocide of millions in the Congo. Next, we're starting a unit on the war against terrorism.

I'm settling into my seat when Mr. Vandenhausler skips to the front of the classroom.

"I have something exciting to announce!" he sings. "I'm squeezing in a special mini-unit on Nepal."

My ears perk up. Nepal is a small country in the Himalayas, right on the border of China.

Mr. Vandenhausler's mustache starts twitching. *Oh no.* That's what happens whenever he's talking blood-and-guts. I brace myself as he adds that we'll learn specifically about how the crown prince shot and killed the king, queen, and seven other members of the royal family during a Friday-night dinner.

"It was such a shock," chirps Mr. Vandenhausler. His mustache is vibrating so much it looks like it's going to pop off his upper lip. "Prince Dipendra was their beloved first born son. No one ever expected he'd do anything as brutal as this."

I think of Byron, of last night, of the phone call from Dean Briggs.

124

By the time the bell rings, my palms are slick with sweat. Mr. Vandenhausler has described the automatic submachine gun the prince used, the order in which the family members were shot, which parts of each body were penetrated. He even projected video clips onto a screen of wailing Nepalese people mourning the loss of their royal family.

The last thing I can imagine doing right now is Shoots and Ladders, but I skipped gym on Monday so I can't ditch twice in a week. I've just entered the locker room when Teri the Tiny Gym Teacher walks in. She's wearing a slate-colored warm-up suit, cross-trainers, and a whistle dangling from a chain around her neck.

"PEEEEE-PULL," Teri bellows, blowing her whistle.

She proceeds to tell us that a fuse blew in the gym, so we're going to be sprinting up and down the hallway instead of doing Shoots and Ladders.

Everyone groans.

"Make sure to wear sneakers," Teri adds. "Because we're going to work you."

I want to strangle myself with a shoelace. I hate doing sprints. I hate being worked. I hate being worked doing sprints a thousand times more than I hate climbing ropes and hanging from rings.

Teri turns to leave, but then stops and blows her whistle again. "I need one volunteer," she shouts.

125

"Someone to record times."

I shoot up my arm faster than a bullet from an automatic submachine gun.

"Good reflexes, Shreves!" says Teri as she hands me a stopwatch and a clipboard.

One point for Shreves.

I get to be Teri the Tiny Gym Teacher's trusty assistant, timing sprints and clutching the clipboard as my classmates heave and pant and sweat their way down the hall. At one point Brie Newhart stumbles into a locker, moaning that she feels faint. Her pale cheeks are splotchy and she looks like she's on the verge of tears.

But even that doesn't make me feel much better.

Third period is French. I don't feel like seeing Froggy, having to smile and act like everything's OK. He's talking to another guy when I walk in, so I give him a quick wave and take my seat.

Ten minutes into class, Mademoiselle Kiefer distributes our weekly quiz. I scan the page. *Passé composé* as far as the eye can see. We have to list the seventeen verbs that use *être* in the past tense. I glance at Froggy and Brie and the other kids chewing their pen caps and scribbling answers. I know I'm going to bomb this quiz, so instead of attempting it, I write:

Why Past Tense Makes Me Tense.

I stare at my potential list, but nothing comes to

mind. My brain feels as empty as the cereal and cracker boxes hidden under my bed.

I spend the rest of the period drawing spirals and three-dimensional boxes on my paper so Mademoiselle Kiefer won't notice I'm not writing and subject me to some form of torturous public humiliation. One time this girl named Alyssa Wu forgot her pen and had to sing "Frère Jacques" in front of the entire class.

When the bell rings, everyone drops the quiz on the corner of Mademoiselle Kiefer's desk. I slip mine into my notebook and dash out the door.

I can't handle another minute of school.

I consider visiting Paul the School Nurse and feigning yet more menstrual cramps, but I already burned a favor with him this week. Ms. Crowley wouldn't condone my skipping chemistry lab. Anyway, I think she's got senior composition fourth period.

I dump my notebooks in my locker and grab my backpack. Then I do something I've never done before. I walk out the front door of Brewster at a little before 11 A.M.

I've left school early for a doctor's appointment or to go home sick, but I've never ditched. There are kids who cut classes on a regular basis—the stoners, the rebels, the trench-coat wearers, but it always sounded vaguely dangerous, definitely not something *I* would ever do.

127

That's why I'm surprised it's so easy to walk out. One moment I'm an inmate at Brewster Penitentiary, and the next I'm strolling up Eighty-fourth Street, the sun on my back, Bunsen burners and bubbling beakers a billion miles away.

I head toward Central Park. It feels like a typical day, except that no one on the street is over five or under twenty. The sidewalks are bustling with stressed-out executive types jabbering on cell phones and sliding on lipstick.

I walk in the direction of the Great Lawn and find a sunny bench to sit on. As I stare up at Belvedere Castle, this little castle in the middle of Central Park, I think of all the movies I've seen where kids ditch school. *Ferris Bueller's Day Off*, of course. And *Mad Love* with Drew Barrymore. If they made a movie about me, I'd want them to call it *Citigurl*.

I pull a notebook out of my bag and am about to scribble that down when I catch sight of my hands. A queasy feeling surges through my body. Last night, when we received the call from Dean Briggs, I was in the middle of painting my fingernails. I'd only polished my left hand when the phone rang.

I stand up and start walking again, but all my ditching-school excitement seems to have disappeared. I feel aimless and lonely and cold. I'd like to go back to our apartment, but Byron is probably moving in at this very moment and I just don't want to be there for that.

Where do you go in New York City when you can't go home? I once read this book about a brother and sister who hide out in the Metropolitan Museum of Art. I always thought it would be more fun to stow away at Macy's. You could sleep in their elaborately made-up beds, watch the gigantic wall of televisions, and take the escalator into the Cellar whenever you're craving munchies.

Munchies. I can go to the movies.

I pull out my wallet. I only have three dollars and forty-seven cents, but my ATM card is tucked behind my school ID. I walk over to Citibank and withdraw money from my savings account. As the receipt is printing, I feel slightly guilty. Mom and Dad are always emphasizing that the one thousand dollars in my bank account is mine, to do with what I want. It's mostly from birthdays and relatives and cat-sitting gigs. But I know they want me to put the money toward taking an Outward Bound course next summer, like Anaïs and Byron did after their sophomore year of high school. Some sort of trailblazing, pooping-in-the-woods occasion. Definitely not my idea of a good time. Not to sound like a city slicker, but I don't like to go too long without TV or a high-speed connection.

I head to the multiplex cinema near Mom's gym.

When I approach the counter, I ask the woman for a ticket to the first movie I see on the digital sign.

"That started ten minutes ago," she says.

I push my money across the counter. She gives me a strange look as she hands me a ticket. Once I'm upstairs, I buy a tub of popcorn with extra butter.

As soon as I'm settled into my seat, I space out. I barely follow the story, but it does the trick of numbing my mind. As the credits roll, I wipe my greasy hands on the chair. Then I dart out of the theater, march into the neighboring one, and slip into an aisle seat.

Midway through my third movie, I run to the bathroom to pee. On the way back, I pay another visit to the concession island. This time I buy nachos with melted cheese, a jumbo pack of Sour Patch Kids, and a Diet Pepsi.

Diet Tip #6: Do not discover that your beloved brother has been found guilty of date rape.

I end up sneaking into seven different movies— some for the whole show, some for random snippets. It's around 9:30 P.M. by the time I finally leave the theater. As I'm walking home, I realize that my stomach aches. My eyes ache. My ears ache. My tongue is raw and my braces are crammed with kernels.

When I arrive home, it's nearly ten. The apartment is quiet and dark. Mom and Dad must be out for the evening. I'm heading down the hallway when I notice a strip of light coming from under Byron's door. My stomach flips nervously as I dash into my bedroom and burrow under my covers without undressing or brushing my teeth.

CHAPTER FOURTEEN

Early in the morning I hear dishes clanking and coffee grinding, but by the time I get out of bed, nobody's home. My parents must be in Connecticut already. They have that big golf tournament next weekend, so they're probably hitting the green early. The door to Byron's room is open. I peek inside. His bed is neatly made and there aren't any suitcases scattered around, nothing out of place.

I still feel popcorn in my braces, so I head into the bathroom and pull out the special dental floss that my orthodontist gave me. As I maneuver a string through my wires, I start thinking that maybe yesterday was just a nightmare, a blunder of my imagination.

I spit some kernel shards into the sink. The next time I see Byron, I'll have to tell him about it. He'll

 132

be shocked by the scenario that my brain conjured up, but he'll quickly find humor in the situation. He'll say something like, *You've been smoking too much weed, Gin.* Then we'll have a good laugh at my expense.

As I swish out my mouth with water, I think of ways to convince Mademoiselle Kiefer to let me make up the French quiz from yesterday. And I bet I can stay after school next week and do the lab on chemical reactions that I missed.

A few minutes later, I'm watching television and peeling an orange. I'm stacking the peels on the coffee table. My eating went a little haywire yesterday, but I've already decided to rein it in again. I'm going to drink two gallons of water today, so much that my pee will be clearer than a mountain creek. And I'll just have some lettuce later, maybe a few honey-nut rice cakes.

The front door unlocks. My tower of orange peels tips over.

"Hey, Gin."

I turn reluctantly, but my throat is too tight to speak.

Byron nods in my direction, but he doesn't smile. He's got a strange look on his face, something I've never seen before. It's a blend of embarrassment and exhaustion. I turn away. I really don't want to see him like this. I wish I could just close my eyes and open them again and have my

133

perfect big brother back.

Dad comes through next. He grunts as he sets a milk crate onto the floor.

"Use your knees, Mike." Mom appears behind him with blazers and shirts draped over her arm.

Dad hunches down, his hands cupped on his knees. "Ginny, what do you say about lending a hand? We've got an entire U-Haul that needs unloading."

I stand up, but I don't say anything. I'm still processing the fact that they're not in the country. They go to Connecticut almost every weekend, rain or shine, sleet or hailstorm. They even went last spring when I won the creative writing award at Brewster's National Honor Society banquet. I ended up sitting at a table with Shannon and her parents instead.

"You might want to grab a sweatshirt," Mom says. "There's a nip in the air."

As I head into my room to get a sweatshirt, I can't stop thinking about how normal my parents just acted. It doesn't seem right. I mean, Byron has been suspended from school for *date rape*. In movies there would be a lot of crying and finger-pointing, maybe a few emotional hugs. So why is my family acting like it's a normal everyday morning?

No one says much during the next hour, as we lug boxes and bags upstairs. At one point, as I'm helping Byron maneuver his futon mattress through the lobby, I try to catch his eye. I'm hoping he'll tell me this has been a huge mistake, but whenever I look at him, he just turns away.

Dad and Byron drive off to return the U-Haul.

Mom and I take the elevator upstairs.

As soon as we get to the apartment, I head into my room and lock the door.

I remain in my bedroom for the rest of the weekend. Mom and Dad knock a few times, but I pretend I'm sleeping. I don't feel like dealing with anything or anyone right now.

The only times I leave are when I'm sure no one's home or when they're all sleeping. Then I dash into the kitchen to scavenge cashews or gingersnaps or Diet Pepsi.

A few times I caught sight of myself in my new mirror, cramming food into my mouth, surrounded by all those diet tips that I stuck into the frame. Finally, on Sunday morning, I removed the tips and crumpled them into the trash.

Now it's Sunday afternoon. I've spent the day dozing and Web surfing and doing homework. For "Ostracism and Oppression," we're reading this amazing book called *Caucasia*. It's about a light-skinned black girl whose mom is running from the law so she has to pretend she's white. Sometimes I wish I could pretend I were somebody else. I don't

135

know who I'd be. Maybe Helen Keller, since she never had to see her reflection in the mirror or hear nasty things that people said about her.

I've kept up with baseball news by visiting ESPN.com. At this point, New York and Seattle have each won once, so there's a decent chance next weekend's game will be happening. Dad hasn't said anything more about giving the tickets away, so I'm still hoping I'll be able to go.

The only human contact I've had are my e-mails with Shannon. I've been writing her nearly every hour. She always writes back, not quite as frequently, but whenever she's online.

It's hard, though. Shannon is currently having a love affair with her Walla Walla friends. Well, not romantic love. I double-checked that in my last e-mail. This was her response:

To: citigurl13
From: goddess_shannon
Date: Sunday, October 13, 3:11 p.m.
Subject: no such luck

Gin—

Regarding your question about love, no such luck. Hunter and Evan are interested in each other. THEY don't know this yet, but Sabrina and I think that once they leave conservative Walla Walla, they'll move to Seattle and profess their undying love for each other. Speaking of

Sabrina, I finally asked about the "Mom" tattoo on her arm. She said it actually spells "Wow" and it's only meant for when she's doing handstands.

How are you? Have you left your bedroom yet?

Love,
Shan

I'm relieved that Shannon isn't getting a boyfriend on top of everything. Even so, it's hard to hear about these great additions to her life. Especially since all I've got is a failed diet and a kink in my lower back from remaining sedentary for the past twenty-nine hours.

Chapter Fifteen

On school days my alarm rings at 6:15 A.M. I keep my clock on my dresser. That means I have to get out of bed to hit the snooze bar, which starts waking me up. Snooze lasts for seven minutes, so I do it twice. If I'm up by 6:29 A.M., in the shower by 6:33 A.M., and out the door by 7 A.M., I can make it to school on time.

As I'm stumbling across my bedroom this morning, I turn the alarm off altogether. I collapse onto my bed again and conk out.

I don't know how much time has passed when I hear a knock on my door.

I roll onto my stomach.

"Can you open up, Virginia?" Mom says from the hallway.

I tug a pillow over my head.

"I gave you your space for the entire weekend.

 138

I just want to talk for a minute."

I roll onto my side.

"Are you awake?" Mom asks. "It's after seven. You're going to have to take a cab to school."

"I'm not going to school," I grumble.

"Please unlock your door and we'll discuss it."

I unlock my door and scramble back to bed before Mom can see me in my shirt and undies. As I dive under the sheets, a cashew jabs into my shoulder blade.

Mom walks in. She's dressed for work, but her hair is damp and she's not wearing any makeup yet.

"You don't feel well?" Mom presses her palm to my forehead. Her hand feels so soft it makes me want to cry.

"No," I whimper.

Mom sits on the edge of my bed. "Does it hurt somewhere specifically?"

I gesture to my stomach. "Maybe here. Sort of all over."

"Do you have any tests today? Anything you can't miss?"

I shake my head. We're starting a unit on atomic theory in chemistry, but I doubt I'll be able to pay attention.

"I've got to get running. I'm meeting Nan for an early yoga class. But I'll give the principal's office a call. It sounds like you need a personal day."

What I really need is a hug. I lift my hands, like a toddler asking to be picked up. Mom leans over, wraps her arms around me, and rocks me back and forth. I can't remember the last time she gave me a hug like this. Tears start running down my cheeks.

"You're having a hard time with this, aren't you?"

I nod and wipe away some tears.

Mom sits back. She inhales through her nose and exhales through her mouth. I call this her ShrinkBreath. It's how I always assume she looks around her patients—calm, cool, composed.

"This isn't an easy ordeal we're facing," she says. "But we all love Byron, so we have to stick by him."

A fresh crop of tears pours out of my eyes. "How could he have done something like that?"

Mom presses her lips tightly together. I have no idea what she's thinking. If some people's faces are open books, Mom's is one of those leather-bound diaries with a lock on the front and a long-lost key.

"I don't know what to say, Virginia." Mom is quiet for a long time, then she takes another ShrinkBreath and says, "Let's just keep going about our lives and pretty soon everything will be back to normal."

I wipe my nose with the back of my hand.

"Do you think you can do that?" Mom asks.

"I'll try," I say quietly.

 140

Mom gives me a quick hug. "I'm glad we had this talk. It's all going to be just fine."

As soon as Mom is gone, I lapse into a fitful sleep. I have bizarre nightmares, one right after the next. I'm having a particularly creepy one about being chased by wild boars when I jolt awake. The clock says 10:21 A.M. I stare out my window at the clouds strangling the tops of buildings.

That's when I hear grunting noises. I get out of bed and press my ear against my door. The grunts become longer, throatier. I grab some sweatpants from my laundry heap and pull them on. Then I tiptoe across the hall and stand in front of Byron's door.

"Grrrrrrr. Grrrrrrrrrr. *AAAARGGGHH*!"

My legs feel weak. Is Byron jacking off in there? Or worse, is he having sex? Oh god, I really didn't want to think about that.

I hear a barbell knock against his floor. I dash into my room and slam the door.

So Byron was lifting weights. While I'm relieved that he wasn't exercising a *lower* portion of his body, I'm still a little shaken.

I slip into my sneakers, grab my wool sweater, and scurry to the elevator.

It's overcast outside with a tinge of winter in the air. I button up my sweater and fold my arms across my chest. As I walk over to Broadway, I realize that I forgot my bankcard. I scrounge around in the change purse attached to my key chain and extract a crinkled five-dollar bill.

I head down to Krispy Kreme. It's about a ten-minute walk. Whenever I pass a college-aged woman on the sidewalk, I find myself wondering if she's the one. No one has given me details, other than what Dad told me after the phone call from Dean Briggs, about it being the girl Byron brought to that Virgins and Sluts party.

The "Hot Now" light is on in the window of Krispy Kreme. I head inside and am comforted by the sweet aroma of doughnuts. As I get into the line, I try to remember her name. I think it was fairly generic. Maybe Amy? Or Abby? Or Ashley?

I order a glazed, a blueberry, and one with chocolate frosting. I've already polished off the glazed doughnut by the time I reach the door.

It's drizzling outside. I lick some sugar off my fingers. I remember Byron's friend, the one who looked like a hamster, mentioning something about the girl. That she was a math major. A cute math major.

As I take a right on Broadway, I try to imagine what happened that night.

Let's say Byron took a shower. He shaved and worked gel through his hair. He only wore a pair of boxers, so he could flaunt his new pecs. But they were nice boxers, like navy blue silk.

I eat the blueberry doughnut. The drizzle is

turning to rain—cold, driving droplets. My wool sweater is getting wet, so it's emitting a putrid animal stench.

By the time Byron met up with her, she was flying high. It's not every day a math major goes out with a rugby god like Byron Shreves. She almost chickened out of wearing the leather bustier and fishnets, but her roommate convinced her to go for it.

They stopped by Hamster Boy's party, had a few beers, and headed over to Virgins and Sluts. They drank. They danced. Maybe it was the spiked punch, but she didn't feel as nervous as before. They started grinding their hips to hip-hop music.

I finish off my last doughnut, crumple the bag, and toss it in a trash bin. It's pouring by this point. My hair is clinging to my ears. My sweatpants are heavy with water. My feet are sloshing in my sneakers. I know it's time to yank the plug on my imagination, but I force myself to watch the next scene.

When the party wound down, Byron invited her back to his room. She'd had a lot of punch, so she knew she shouldn't go. But her brain was too murky and Byron's aftershave smelled too good.

Maybe Byron lit candles. Maybe he played jazz. Either way, they started making out. At first, she thought it felt good, but soon she noticed that Byron was moving really quickly. They'd barely

started kissing when one of his hands undid her bustier, the other pushed down her fishnets. She asked him to slow down, but she was so drunk that her words were garbled.

The next thing she knew, Byron was rolling on a condom. She said no, but he was already inside of her. She told him to stop, but his eyes were closed as he pumped into a body that didn't feel like hers anymore.

"Are you OK, sweetheart?"

I blink several times. My vision is blurred, but I can make out a middle-aged woman with a concerned look on her face. Until she stopped me, I hadn't realized I'd been bawling my head off.

"Can I help you?" she asks.

"No," I say. "I'll be OK."

She nods reluctantly, so I dodge into a nearby Starbucks and head for the bathroom.

I glance at my reflection. My hair is drenched. My saliva and tears and snot are streaming together.

I dry my face with a scratchy paper towel.

This is so confusing. For as long as I can remember, I've looked up to Byron more than anyone in the world. If he's the sun, I'm a planet revolving around him. Everything I've done in my life—from where I chose to go to high school to how I feel about myself—has been because of my big brother.

But now that Byron has done something this

144

horrible to a girl, I don't know what to make of anything. I mean, if you take away the sun's light, the planets won't know where to go or what to do.

I start sobbing again. As I lean against the filthy bathroom wall, I remind myself to be numb.

It's the only way I'll be able to carry on.

CHAPTER SIXTEEN

"Where were you yesterday?" Froggy asks as I hang my jacket in my locker.

It's Tuesday morning. I wanted to take another personal day, but Mom reminded me about our "keep going about our lives" talk. So here I am, keeping going.

"I didn't see you in French, but I waited on the front stoop anyway." Froggy leans against the locker next to mine. "I waited for more than twenty minutes."

I fish a few textbooks out of my backpack. "I was sick."

"Again?" Froggy asked as he snaps and unsnaps his three-ring binder.

I don't respond.

"So you'll be there next Monday?"

When Froggy says that, my stomach does a

 146

flippy thing. I think about how his neck smells up close and what it feels like to nuzzle my face against his lips. But then I get a sharp pain in my gut. I don't want to think about fooling around right now. I don't want to think about anything that will remind me of Byron's ordeal. I don't want to think about it so much that if a certain sexy green-eyed shortstop came up to me right now and said I was the love of his life and he wanted to elope to the Bahamas with me, I'd tell him I was a nun.

"No," I say.

"What do you mean?"

I stare into the dark void of my locker. Last year Shannon and I stayed after school to line our lockers with wallpaper and hang up pictures and postcards, but this year I didn't do anything at all. "I won't be there next Monday."

"Are you saying it's over?" Froggy's voice cracks on the word "over."

Just then Mr. Moony hobbles by. He's got a Band-Aid across the bridge of his nose. He hasn't been in top form these days, colliding with lockers, tripping down stairs, sleeping in class. But his song archives are still as sharp as shattered glass.

The next thing I know, Mr. Moony starts rasping, "*Froggy went a-courtin' and he did ride, a-huh, a-huh.*"

People stare at us. Froggy drops his notebook and scoops it up again. Normally, I would have croaked from mortification, but I'm instructing every muscle in my body, every cell, every emotion to be numb.

As soon as Mr. Moony is out of earshot, I turn to a red-cheeked Froggy and say, "It can't be over because it never began."

Froggy takes a step backward. "So what was the last month, Virginia? Wasn't that anything to you?"

I want Froggy to go away. I need Froggy to go away. If he hangs around for another second, my self-inflicted anesthesia is going to wear off.

"Did you think that was something?" I ask curtly. "Because you sure didn't act like it when we were in school."

Froggy tweaks his nose a few times. "I thought that's how you wanted it. I mean, you always seemed to…"

I cut him off. "Well, *stop* thinking, OK?"

Then I grab my notebooks, slam my locker, and march away, leaving Froggy rubbing his nose and staring in my wake.

I can barely pay attention in global studies. That's probably a good thing because Mr. Vandenhausler is knee-deep in the carnage in Kathmandu. As soon as the bell rings, he announces that we're going to learn the process by which they inhumed the bodies of the Nepalese royal family. I'm not sure what "inhumed" means, but judging by the amount that his mustache is twitching, I don't *want* to know.

I keep replaying the interaction with Froggy in my head. I was just a total bitch to him, which he didn't deserve in the slightest. But I couldn't help it. The idea of any guy coming near me makes my skin crawl. It reminds me too much of Byron and that girl—two things I totally don't want to think about right now.

At lunchtime I grab a pack of Hostess Cupcakes and snarf them on the way up to Ms. Crowley's office. I stop briefly in the second-floor bathroom to toss the wrapper. I'd never hang out in a stall again—too many bad memories from the Bri-girls episode—but I still come in for a quick pee or to remove some food from my braces.

As soon as I walk in, I hear movement in a stall. I freeze when I notice that the person in the stall is wearing high-heeled magenta boots. Those are Brie Newhart's boots. She's the only girl in school who has them because they came all the way from Paris.

My first thought is: What is Brie doing up here? She always spends lunch period at the sophomore royalty table—flanked by cute boys, far from the trash bins, close to the exits. Besides, there's a bathroom right near the cafeteria.

My second thought is: Stop thinking thought #1 and get out of here! Brie Newhart is the last person

I feel like seeing right now.

I toss my cupcake wrapper in the trash and hurry out of the bathroom.

"I've missed you these past few days," Ms. Crowley says. She's sitting at her desk, marking up an essay test with a red pen. "Were you braving the cafeteria?"

"Nope." I sink into the spare chair. "I was out sick."

"Are you feeling better?"

"I guess."

"Did being sick have anything to do with your diet?"

I think about the masses of sugar and chocolate and carbs I've consumed these past five days. I think about how I crept into the kitchen last night and tore the Food Police off the fridge.

"No." I sigh. "My diet is over."

"What happened?"

I gnaw at a hangnail on my thumb.

"Other stuff going on in your life?"

I nod.

"And eating helps you deal with it?"

I nod again.

"I've been there," Ms. Crowley says. "All I can say is, you'll figure it out eventually. It has to be the right time in your life. You don't want to diet to make someone else happy." Ms. Crowley is quiet for a moment. "Do you want to talk about it?"

 150

"Talk about what?"

"What else is going on in your life."

I yank at the hangnail with my teeth, so hard that it tears off a strip of skin. I wish I could tell Ms. Crowley about Byron being kicked out of college and how I'm so confused about everything. But I can't. Byron was a star student at Brewster, four-time MBS winner and overall legend. So who am I to drag his reputation through the mud? Besides, it's a Shreves family policy to not talk about our dirty laundry—in public and usually not even in private. It's sort of like if you don't discuss it, it didn't happen.

"No thanks." I grab a tissue from Ms. Crowley's desk and dab it on my thumbnail, which is dotted with blood. Then I repeat what Mom said the other morning. "It's all going to be just fine."

Ms. Crowley looks unconvinced.

"Really," I say, flashing her my best imitation of a smile.

To: citigurl13
From: goddess_shannon
Date: Tuesday, October 15, 5:51 p.m.
Subject: something to be thankful for

Virginia—
How are you coping? I hate to think of you crying outside in the rain. I wish I could be there for you.

Guess what?

I MAY BE SOON!!!!!

Liam just got some royalties from the shoelace book, so he and Nina have decided to live it up. We're going to Seattle for Thanksgiving. Three nights. Two rooms at the Claremont Hotel. One room for them and one for us.

Us = YOU AND ME!!!!!!!!!!!!!!!!!!

My parents said your parents would only have to get the plane tix and they'd cover the rest.

PLEASE SAY YES!

Love,
Shannon

To: goddess_shannon
From: citigurl13
Date: Tuesday, October 15, 5:53 p.m.
Subject: ???

Don't you want to bring your new friends?

To: citigurl13
From: goddess_shannon
Date: Tuesday, October 15, 5:56 p.m.
Subject: !!!

Don't be an idiot, Virginia.

So ... can you come?

To: goddess_shannon
From: citigurl13
Date: Tuesday, October 15, 5:57 p.m.
Subject: YES

Yes! Yes! Yes! Yes! Yes!

CHAPTER SEVENTEEN

"No."

"Mom, come on. Please. *Pleeeeeeeease.*"

"Absolutely not."

"Why not?" I sink to my knees and clasp my hands into the praying position. I'm not religious, but there are times in life when God comes in handy—taking off in airplanes, final exams, weekend jaunts to Seattle. "Is it because you don't like Shannon's parents? Because they're really nice if only you'd give them a—"

"Get up, Virginia. I don't know where you got that crazy notion about Liam Newman and Nina Malloy. They're perfectly decent people. I don't want you to go to Seattle because there's too much going on right now. Besides, I've already invited the Lowensteins and Nan Grossman, so I want to have as normal a Thanksgiving as possible."

I lean against the kitchen counter where Mom is mincing basil leaves. "What's the"—I make quotation marks with my fingers—"'too much going on?' Are you talking about Byron?"

Mom sweeps the basil into a measuring cup and doesn't say a word.

I pluck up a leaf and pop it into my mouth. "What about what you said, about how we have to"—I curl my fingers into quotes again—"'keep going about our lives and pretty soon everything will be back to normal?' If that's the case, then why should Byron's ordeal affect what *I* do for Thanksgiving?"

Mom slams the knife onto the cutting board. "What's gotten into you? You're starting to sound like Anaïs."

"I'm sorry. I just don't think it's fair."

Mom slips on her reading glasses and squints at the cookbook. "Life isn't always fair."

"So why do I have to get the brunt of it?"

"You should meet some of my patients," Mom says. "Then you'd see teenagers who've had it hard. Not being able to go to Seattle for the weekend isn't getting the brunt of *anything*."

I grab another piece of basil, head into my bedroom, and slam the door. This leaf must not have been washed yet because I wind up with a mouthful of sand.

This only contributes to my week from hell. It's

Saturday afternoon. Ever since Shannon's e-mail, I've been begging my parents to let me go to Seattle. I want to go so badly it hurts. Mom nixed it from the start—too much going on, need a normal Thanksgiving, blah, blah, blah. At first, Dad suggested using his frequent flier miles and arranging for a free flight, but Mom vetoed that idea. Later that evening I heard them arguing, though I'm not sure whether it was about Seattle or all the other things going on. There's been a lot of tension around the apartment recently.

Over the past few days, details of Byron's date rape have been trickling out. No one has talked with me about it, but my parents and Byron have been having late-night conversations in the living room. I've developed supersonic listening skills, which work especially well when I'm sitting on the floor of my bedroom with the door cracked open ever so slightly.

On Tuesday night I was reminded that the girl's name is Annie Mills. She's a junior at Columbia. And she's from Saskatchewan. I knew that was somewhere in Canada, but when I was in global studies the next morning, I flipped to the page in my textbook with the world map. I was surprised to discover how far west it was, all the way above Montana.

On Wednesday night I overheard Byron admit to my parents that he slept with Annie on the night

 156

of the Virgins and Sluts party. Byron was explaining how Annie had reported the incident to the Office of Sexual Misconduct rather than going to the police. From there, it all happened quickly. They convened a panel of students who heard the case and voted to suspend Byron for the rest of the semester. Dean Briggs seconded the decision. It sounds like Byron has thirty days to appeal. I was falling through my door by this point, straining to catch every word.

I heard Mom ask Byron about the likelihood of winning an appeal. I couldn't make out a response, so I inched forward on my butt until I was in the hallway.

"I'm not sure," Byron said. "I drank way too much that night. We started fooling around and it went too far. How can I say whether it was consensual? I couldn't remember anything the next morning."

Neither Mom nor Dad said anything. I wished they would yell at him, tell him that, wasted or sober, he had no right to force himself onto Annie Mills.

But then Byron said, "Let's say I made a mistake. Will I have to pay for it forever?"

I could hear little sobs. I slid to the end of the hallway and peeked into the living room. Byron was sitting on the couch with his head bowed. Mom and Dad were on either side of him.

Mom rested her hand on his shoulder. "Everything's going to be OK," she said.

Dad tousled Byron's hair. "That's right, son."

I rubbed my knuckles against my braces until I shredded the skin.

On Thursday my parents took Byron to their lawyer so they could get a professional opinion on whether he should appeal. I didn't find this out until my nightly snooping session. I was crouched at the end of the hallway when I heard Dad say that he agreed with the lawyer, that an appeal was probably not the best idea.

"It could just open you up to a stronger penalty," Dad said.

"Or provoke the girl to take it up with the police department," Mom added.

I picked at a small scab on my knuckle where my braces had torn the skin the night before. I wanted to chime in that "the girl" has a name and it's Annie Mills.

By Friday Byron descended into a depression. He was just getting out of bed when I got home from school. I half waved into the kitchen, where he was slurping down a bowl of Cheerios, but I didn't say anything and neither did he. That's how it's been since he moved back. To be honest, I don't know what to say to him. *It'll be all right?* Not for Annie Mills. *I'm sorry?* For Annie Mills, but not for you. *How's the weather?* It sucks—cold, gray, and drizzly.

The skies finally cleared last night, but even so, Mom and Dad bailed on their golf tournament. The Yankees and Seattle are three and two in the playoffs. This afternoon's game could determine who's going to the World Series. Dad decided to take Byron as an attempt to bolster his spirits. When I learned that, I was stunned. That's the game *I* had originally been invited to. I'd wanted to go so badly I could taste it. Besides, my parents have been anticipating their golf tournament for months.

But what really blew me away was what happened with Mom. As soon as Dad and Byron left for Yankee Stadium, she dashed outside and returned an hour later with bags of groceries and a loaf of Italian bread wrapped in white paper.

I watched as Mom washed her hands and rolled back her sleeves. Then she unpacked fresh mozzarella, a bunch of basil, tomatoes, garlic, and a slab of meat. I was completely speechless. Mom denounced cooking when Anaïs left for college five years ago.

"I've paid my motherly dues," she'd said as soon as they returned from dropping my sister off at Dartmouth. Then Mom slapped a pile of take-out menus onto the kitchen counter. "We'll let the delivery guy pick up the slack."

Over the past five years, Mom has only cooked

on special occasions, like Thanksgiving or Christmas or if we're having company over.

But I can't for the life of me figure out how this constitutes a special occasion.

"Phyl, you've outdone yourself!" Dad exclaims. He drains his first glass of red wine and pours himself a second.

I eye Dad taking a long swig. Ever since Byron's been home, Dad's been drinking more than usual.

"I thought a home-cooked meal would cheer everyone up," Mom says. "But it doesn't look like you need it."

Dad and Byron were in high spirits when they arrived home an hour ago. I boycotted watching the game for obvious reasons, but when they came through the door singing "New York, New York," I knew we were headed to the World Series.

"To the Yankees." Dad raises his wineglass.

Mom and Byron clink with him.

I survey the candlelit table. Mom made veal Parmesan, linguine, and a mixed green salad. I only took a sliver of meat and a heap of salad, no bread or pasta. I still act like I'm on a diet when I'm around my parents, which is such a joke because I've been gaining weight again. I can only fit into my Fat Pants, the ones I save in the back of my closet for when I'm really bloated.

We're just finishing dinner when Dad says,

 160

"Guess what Byron and I were discussing this afternoon?"

"What's that?" Mom picks at the lettuce on her plate. In the past week, Mom has been munching a lot—pretzels and Veggie Booty and even some of Dad's olive oil potato chips. Last night Dad joked about Mom plumping up for winter. When he said that, Mom spit her mouthful of chips into a paper towel. Now I guess she's back to her usual regimen of lettuce and water.

Byron wipes his mouth with his napkin. "I'd have to double-check with your lawyer about the legal implications, but I'm thinking about going to Paris until the beginning of next semester."

"When would you leave?" Mom asks.

"As soon as possible. In the next two or three weeks."

I do some quick calculations. That would have Byron out of town by mid-November. I set down my fork. "But what about—"

"I think it's a great idea," Mom says, cutting me off. "You've always wanted to spend time in Paris and you could probably use the change of scenery."

I clench my fists. "But what about Thanksgiv—"

"Virginia," Mom says. "We're talking about completely different circumstances."

"But—"

Dad jumps in. "Hey, Ginny, maybe I could take

161

you on that shopping spree we were talking about, get you something nice to wear for Thanksgiving dinner."

I shrug. "I don't know."

Dad has this lopsided grin on his face. I think he's had too much to drink tonight. "Have you gotten any closer to the body goal that Mom was talking about?"

I stare at my empty plate.

"I'm going to take off," Byron says, pushing back his chair.

As Byron heads toward his bedroom, Mom raises her eyebrows at me. "I hope you're still taking this diet seriously."

Dad rises from his chair, using the edge of the table to steady himself.

"Make us proud," he says.

Mom gathers together some dishes. "Make *yourself* proud."

They head into the kitchen. I hear water running. I stare at the flames flickering atop the candlesticks.

How is it that Byron is allowed to go to Paris for Thanksgiving and I can't visit my best friend who I haven't seen in over three months? He gets kicked out of college for date rape and still gets a Yankee playoff game *and* a change of scenery? All I've done is gain a few pounds and suddenly I'm the one being penalized.

I feel bile stinging my throat, anger seeping through my body. Before I know it, I'm holding my hand over a candle. It's warm on my fingertip. I lower it until my pointer is touching the flame. I can smell the stench of burning flesh.

I hear Mom approaching the dining room so I pull my hand away.

"What's that smell?" she asks. "Does something smell funny in here?"

I don't answer. She leans over and blows out the candles.

As Mom heads into the kitchen again, I rock back and forth, cradling my hand in my lap. My finger is searing in pain. But at least the pain is concentrated in one spot rather than dominating my entire body.

CHAPTER EIGHTEEN

I'm having a hard time writing to Anaïs. Her twenty-third birthday is on November fifteenth. Mom is putting together a care package to send to Africa, so I want to include a letter. It'll take a few weeks to arrive in Ouagadougou, the capital of Burkina Faso, and several more days to make it to her rural hut.

There are two reasons why writing this letter is impossible. For one, my finger is burned pretty badly. It's been eleven days and it's still raw and blistery and oozing. It hurts all the time, especially when I'm on the computer. That's why I'm hand-writing Anaïs's letter. For the past hour, I've been sitting on my bed with a stack of stationery on my lap. I've churned out four attempts, but I keep crumpling them up and tossing them onto my rug.

Which ties into the second reason why this is so

 164

difficult. When I told Mom I wanted to include a letter in my sister's package, she asked that I not mention Byron being home from Columbia.

"Keep it upbeat," Mom said. "Anaïs is witnessing disease and poverty on a daily basis. The last thing she needs is something else to worry about."

I was tempted to say, *So you want me to lie?*, but I kept my mouth shut.

I'm already on Mom's bad side because I've been begging on a daily basis to go to Seattle. It's three weeks away, so I'm still clinging to a shred of hope that she'll change her mind.

But that doesn't make it any easier to write to Anaïs. In my first four attempts, I embellished on my life so lavishly I could have won a Pulitzer Prize for fiction. They all made me queasy. Recently, I've been finding it harder to pretend that everything is A-OK.

I begin attempt #5.

Dear Anaïs,

Here's a juicy piece of news! I had a fling this fall. His name is Froggy Welsh the Fourth. He's also a sophomore at Brewster. He also knows every word to the "Friends" theme song. At first, I didn't think he was that cute, but the more I got to know him, the more he grew on me. Has that ever happened to you? Well, it doesn't matter because those days are over. Byron date-raped a girl and now I'm repulsed by sex or anything leading up to it. I told Froggy to get lost and now he won't even look in my direction or talk to me...

I fling the paper onto my carpet and embark on my sixth attempt.

Dear Anaïs,

Tomorrow is Halloween! I've decided to go as the woman who sings the arias at the Metropolitan Opera. Yes, the FAT LADY. I was on a diet, but those days are over. I'm the heaviest I've ever been. Even when I'm wearing my Fat Pants, I have to keep the top button undone. I've been pigging out so much, ever since Byron got kicked out of Columbia for date rape and...

Another crumpled letter on the floor. I take a deep breath and flex my hand a few times.

Dear Anaïs,

The Yankees won the World Series!! Normally, I'd be freaking out, but those days are over. My heart wasn't in it this year. I watched a few of the games with Dad and Byron, but every so often I'd glance at our brother and I'd be filled with intense anger. How can a date rapist casually munch a handful of Dutch pretzels and sip a beer when a girl's life has been destroyed?

I crumple attempt #7.

Then I grab my jacket and walk over to Cardeology.

 166

I check out a dozen cards before finding the right one. It's got two smiling girls on the front, one with blond hair and one with brown hair. They're embracing each other amidst a field of wildflowers. On the inside it says *Hugs and kisses on your birthday*.

When I get home, I write:

Dear Anaïs,
   I hope all is well in Burkina Faso.
   I miss you.
   Love,
     Gin

I'm sitting in the auditorium waiting for the annual awards ceremony to begin. They hold it on Halloween every year. It was originally intended to be a costume contest, but it's evolved into an occasion to spotlight Brewster's best and brightest. This is the day they give out plaques to all the Model Brewster Students.

Woo-hoo. I'm sure I'm totally in the running.

We had to report to our last period class before heading downstairs. Most likely Brewster's ploy to get us to climb more stairs. I'm sitting next to Alyssa Wu, the girl who had to sing "Frère Jacques" in French that time. She's in all my classes. She's nice, but definitely a strange bird. She's got long hair, almost down to her butt, and tiny bangs snipped across the top of her forehead. And she's always knitting, even at her desk.

I was relieved to get out of math today. Math is my second favorite subject, after language arts, but my mind has been wandering a lot recently. It's actually to the point where my grades are starting to slip.

I scan the crowd. The right quadrant of the auditorium is the popular section. Brie Newhart is dressed as a queen, complete with a tiara and a velvet cloak lined with faux fur. Brinna and Briar are wearing skintight cat suits and headbands with pointy ears. They must see Halloween as a prime opportunity to flaunt their own personal skeletons.

The front row is faculty and staff. Mademoiselle Kiefer is attempting to flirt with the sexy male physics teacher. The only problem is, he's ogling Teri the Tiny Gym Teacher, who's dressed as a cheerleader. I'm trying to determine whether Teri is shaking her pompoms at the physics teacher when I spot Froggy.

He's seated to my left, surrounded by a group of his friends. That's when I notice that Froggy is sitting next to a ninth-grader named Sarah. She has a ski-jump nose and a slight overbite, giving her an overall rabbity look. I tighten my fists, even though it causes extreme pain to my burnt finger. I know I have no claim to Froggy. We're not even talking anymore. But it's not like I want to see him with another girl.

"Byron Shreves is your older brother, isn't he?"

I turn to face Alyssa. She's knitting an orange-and-brown square.

"Yeah," I say, tentatively.

"Didn't he win an MBS award every year he was here?"

I nod.

"That's impressive," Alyssa says. "I've heard he's a great guy."

"Who said that?"

"Lots of people."

"Don't believe everything you hear."

Alyssa misses a stitch.

The principal strides onto the stage. She's wearing a wizard's cape, half-moon glasses, and a silver beard. I think she's dressed as Dumbledore, the headmaster in the Harry Potter books. I'm relieved when she taps her wand onto the microphone to signal the beginning of the awards ceremony.

The crosstown bus doesn't come for fifteen minutes, so I decide to walk home across Central Park. The sky is bright blue and there's a chilly wind slicing down the avenues. I hug my arms across my chest and keep a fast pace.

Of course, Brie Newhart won an MBS award. She got it for being an overall positive addition to our school. She delivered such a tear-filled acceptance speech—half of which was in French—you'd think she'd won an Oscar. Mademoiselle Kiefer actually gave her a standing ovation.

They also presented MBS awards for athletics and community service. Every other school does awards in the spring, but Brewster has this theory that if you highlight exemplary talent at the beginning of the year, it will raise the bar for the rest of us slackers. But as I slouched in my chair and listened to how Hannah Hajost built houses for Habitat for Humanity and Kyle Bartz was the Most Valuable Runner on the varsity cross-country team, it only made me want to curl up and take a nap.

Just when I thought the torture was over, the principal announced that she had some exciting news.

"One of our sophomores has just won an extremely competitive graphic design award," the principal said. "Over a hundred high-schoolers submitted designs and the prize went to…"

I held my breath, distinctly remembering that day back in September when Froggy told me about a design competition he was entering.

"Froggy Welsh the Fourth!" she exclaimed, flapping the sides of her cape like wings. "Please join me on stage for a special MBS award, young man."

Everyone applauded, but Froggy was stuck to his chair. After a few moments, Sarah tugged him to his feet and shoved him down the aisle. The principal shook Froggy's hand and told him to continue making Brewster proud.

I enter Central Park near the Met. The air is freezing, but I'm pretty wound up, so it feels good to be walking home.

Making people proud. Is that what life is about? That's what Mom and Dad told me a few weeks ago. Make them proud. Make myself proud. But I've spent my whole life trying to win their praise and where has it gotten me?

As I walk along the Great Lawn, I pass the bench where I sat the day I ditched school, the day after I found out about Byron.

Take my brother. He gets kicked out of college for date rape and, as Alyssa Wu pointed out, he still has a great reputation. Or Brie. She acts like a total ice queen and she still wins an MBS award.

I'm walking faster by this point, my heels clomping against the path. What if for one second I didn't care what people thought of me? What if I weren't so eager to please Mom and Dad? What if I didn't always try to blend in, go with the flow, be the good, obedient fat girl?

What on earth would I do?

As I reach Central Park West, the answer hits me as certain as the gusts slapping my cheeks.

I'd visit Shannon Iris Malloy-Newman.

I'd go to Seattle for Thanksgiving.

There's a Liberty Travel two blocks from our building. I've walked by it a million times, but I've never gone inside. As I step through the door, I'm greeted by a bored-looking guy digging through a bowl of Halloween goodies.

"Hey," he says as he nibbles off the top of a candy corn.

I glance at the cardboard witches, the plastic jack-o'-lanterns, the cotton spider webs obscuring posters of Jamaican beaches.

"How much would a plane ticket to Seattle cost?" I ask.

He decapitates another candy corn. "That all depends on when you want to go."

I rub my hands together. "Over Thanksgiving."

He wheels his chair around so he's facing the computer. I can't believe I'm here. As he begins typing, I'm tempted to bolt back onto Broadway.

"It'll be a minute." The man pushes the bowl of candies in my direction. "Why don't you take a seat?"

I pop a sugary pumpkin in my mouth and settle down across from him. I have to clutch the sides of my chair to keep from running away.

"Were you thinking Wednesday to Sunday?" he asks.

 172

That would mean missing a day of school. I'd better not give my parents any extra reasons to say no. "Is there anything that leaves on Thanksgiving Day?"

"I've got a flight leaving LaGuardia at eight-forty-two on Thursday morning. It transfers in Denver, which will get you to the Sea-Tac Airport at two-thirty-five that afternoon."

I scoop up a few candy corns and mash them between my molars. "How much is it?"

"With all applicable taxes, it comes to four hundred and fifty-eight dollars."

I'm quiet for a second. That's nearly half my savings account.

"Do you want me to ticket it?" he asks.

"Can you hold it for a while?"

"Sure," he says. "But I'd recommend moving quickly because there are only a few seats left on that flight. It's a holiday weekend."

I spell out my name for him and then jog to a nearby Citibank. If I'm going to do this, I'd better do it now. I enter my PIN number and take out five hundred dollars. My hands are trembling as I count out ten crisp fifty-dollar bills.

This is my money, I keep telling myself. *Mom and Dad have always said I can do whatever I want with it.*

Twenty minutes later I exit Liberty Travel with plane tickets in my hand. As I walk home, I want

173

to tell every person I pass, *I'm going to Seattle three weeks from today! I'm spending Thanksgiving with my best friend! Can you believe it? Can you* fucking *believe it?!*

I know nothing major has changed. Brie Newhart is still an MBS. Byron will still be moping around the apartment, resisting my parents' attempts to cheer him up. I'm still wearing Fat Pants with the button open and two inches unzipped.

No, nothing major has changed.

But everything feels different.

CHAPTER NINETEEN

I still haven't told my parents about Seattle. Today is November fifteenth. Six days before Thanksgiving. Six days before I'm scheduled to board a westbound flight. I have to tell them soon. I've *almost* done it about fifty times these past few weeks, but just as I'm readying the muscles in my mouth, I wimp out. I'm afraid they'll simply say, *No, absolutely not, and—by the way—you're grounded for life.* Until I devise a more foolproof plan, I've kept it a secret.

The plane tickets are stashed in my cedar box in my top dresser drawer. Every morning I take them out and hold them in my hands. I do the same thing as soon as I get home from school and right before I go to bed. I doubt I'll be allowed to actually *use* the tickets, but it makes me feel better to know that for one brief instant, I was bold and courageous.

175

It was a mistake to waste my money on them. *An impulse buy.* That's what Mom called it the time she purchased an eight-hundred-dollar dress from Saks. But she went back the next day and returned it. I bought nonrefundable tickets, so I'll just have to suck up the loss.

It's not like I've completely given up yet. I'm planning to tell my parents tonight. Everyone will be in a good mood because it's Anaïs's twenty-third birthday. Dad is bringing home dessert and we're going to celebrate in her honor.

Around 9 P.M. Dad lifts a carrot cake out of its box and sets it in the middle of the table. I poke twenty-three candles into the thick white frosting.

"Byron?" Mom shouts from the kitchen, where she's scavenging the freezer for the nonfat sorbet that she's going to have instead of cake.

No answer from my brother.

I add a twenty-fourth candle for good luck.

"Byron?" Mom sets some mango sorbet on the table. "Don't you want to come to Anaïs's birthday party?"

Byron peeks his head out of his bedroom. "I'm not up for it tonight. Go ahead without me."

No one says a word, but it dampens the mood. We light the candles and sing "Happy Birthday," but the song trails off somewhere in the middle.

That exemplifies the gloom that's pervaded our apartment these past few weeks, ever since Byron got depressed again. He mopes around the apartment all day. I don't even think he's lifting weights anymore. It all started when my parents' lawyer recommended that Byron not go to Paris. Something about how he should give Columbia the impression that he's remorseful about this incident rather than viewing it as vacation time.

"Why should Columbia care which continent I'm remorseful on?" Byron asked Mom as soon as he got off the phone with the lawyer.

I was sitting at my computer, surfing the Web for a site on how to get your parents to agree to something they've already nixed. I was tempted to call into the other room, *I doubt ANNIE MILLS gets to decide on which continent she nurses her wounded soul.*

I think Byron is also depressed because the reality of his situation is finally hitting him. One day he was Big Man on Campus and now his life has come to a screeching halt. Usually when my brother is home, the phone rings off the hook—friends inviting him to nightclubs, girls asking him to movies, guys organizing an Ultimate Frisbee game. But now, hardly anyone calls for Byron. Mom says it's because they're all away at school, wrapped up in their own respective lives. But I think they've gotten wind of what Byron did to Annie Mills and they're as repulsed as I am about it.

As I lick the cream-cheese frosting off my fork, I review my strategy for telling my parents about Seattle. I've decided to take the casual route, so I don't raise their defenses. As in: *Hey, guys, I'm going to Seattle next Thursday morning*, the way Dad announces last-minute business trips.

Mom must have read my mind. She spoons some sorbet into her mouth and says, "Well, the upside of Byron not going to Paris is that the four of us will be in town for Thanksgiving. Too bad Anaïs can't be here, too."

I choke on my frosting.

"Are you OK?" Dad asks.

I nod as I chug a glass of milk.

Mom starts rambling on about how she's determined to make homemade cranberry jelly and smooth mashed potatoes.

I help myself to another slice of carrot cake.

To: citigurl13
From: goddess_shannon
Date: Friday, November 15, 9:56 p.m.
Subject: brainstorm

Gin—

Why don't you tell your parents that you bought a one-way ticket to Seattle and you're not coming home? That way, when they discover that you're flying roundtrip, they'll be so relieved that they'll allow you to come. By the way, Liam and Nina have offered to call your parents and reassure them that the plan is legit.

Love,
Shan

To: goddess_shannon
From: citigurl13
Date: Friday, November 15, 10:31 p.m.
Subject: re: brainstorm

Shan—

If I tell my parents that I'm going to Seattle, I may as well have bought a one-way ticket because there won't be a home waiting for me after the weekend. Please thank Liam and Nina for their offer, but I'm afraid there's nothing anyone can do to convince them.

Love,
Gin

P.S. Maybe you should invite Sabrina to Seattle.

Chapter Twenty

On Monday morning, as I reach into my cedar box for the plane tickets, I pull out the pictures that Byron and I took in a photo booth at Grand Central Station a few years ago. My jaw clenches up when I see them. It's hard to look at us, our arms slung around each other as we cross our eyes and flash our teeth. We'd just come back from spending the night with my parents out in Connecticut. Byron had to return to the city for an early rugby practice the following morning, so I offered to take the train with him and keep him company.

I tuck the photos back in the box and pull out the plane tickets.

Ms. Crowley is the only person in New York City who knows about Seattle. I broke down and told her after she grilled me for five lunch periods in a row. She kept commenting that I had a secret

 180

smile on my face.

"Is there a new guy in your life?" she asked last Tuesday.

"Not a new one or an old one," I said.

Ms. Crowley nodded sympathetically. I'd recently told her about Froggy. Not the graphic details, but just that there used to be something going on and now he'll barely look in my direction.

"Have you taken up witchcraft?" Ms. Crowley asked on Wednesday. "Do you know where rainbows come from? Are you getting a ladybug tattooed onto your ankle?"

I laughed. "No, no, and *definitely* no."

On Thursday, when I finally told her that I secretly bought plane tickets to Seattle, she said, "You are a brave woman."

"Brave enough to throw away five hundred bucks."

"Don't be so quick to doubt yourself, Virginia."

"Whatever," I said.

When I go to Ms. Crowley's office today, there's a Post-it stuck to her computer monitor:

V—

Did you tell them over the weekend??

I'm in a meeting. See you tomorrow!

E. C.

I reach into my backpack and pull out my math notebook and a poppy-seed bagel with cream cheese. I've just conquered the congruent triangle when the bell rings. I head into the second-floor bathroom to pick the poppy seeds out of my braces.

As I open the door, I hear puking noises. The toilet flushes and then there's silence. I'm about to ask if the person is OK when I peek under the stall.

I suck in my breath.

High-heeled magenta boots all the way from Paris.

This is the fourth time I've seen Brie Newhart's boots in this bathroom in the past few weeks. Until now, I'd never really thought about it.

I stand there for a second, adding two and two together. *Second-floor bathroom. Far from the cafeteria. Puking. Skeletally skinny. Feeling faint in gym class.*

Could Brie have an eating disorder?

I mean, she and the other Bri-girls are always bragging about dieting and exercise, but that's one thing. Throwing up your tater tots on a daily basis is another.

I hurry back into the hallway. Maybe I'm blowing the whole thing out of proportion.

Then again, she *did* say that if she looked like me, she'd kill herself.

And I know from Mom that if an eating

 182

disorder gets out of control, that's exactly what can happen.

I'm still thinking about Brie on the bus ride home from school. I can't get those vomiting sounds out of my head. I know I have every reason to hate her—she's gorgeous, she's popular, she treats me like a pigeon dropping, she used her cell phone to bust Froggy in French class. But I actually feel sorry for her. I mean, we're on opposite ends of the weight spectrum, but I know what it's like to hate your body so much that you want to hurt it.

When I come through the front door, I hear the TV blaring inside. I glance into the living room. Byron is conked out on the couch, his hair oily, his face coated in stubble. He has a half-eaten bag of Oreos nestled into the crook of his arm. I get a pang in my stomach when I remember how we used to split open Oreos, fill them with ice cream, and make cookie sandwiches.

These are the kind of things I can only think about when Byron is sleeping. When he's awake, all I want to do is shake him by the shoulders and ask how he could have treated a girl so badly.

An hour later I'm sitting on my bed, attempting to concentrate on manganese and titanium and unununium. My chemistry textbook is propped open in my lap. We have a huge test tomorrow on transition elements on the periodic table, but I keep spacing out, wondering if Brie is bulimic, how I'll tell my parents about Seattle, whether Annie Mills celebrates Thanksgiving even though she's Canadian, who in their right mind would name a metal "unununium."

There's a knock on my door.

"Come in," I shout.

Mom walks in. She's wearing a tailored black pantsuit. And she must have gotten her hair touched up today because it's browner than usual.

"How was school?" she asks.

"Fine."

"Anything interesting happen?"

"Not really."

"Do you have a lot of homework?"

"Some," I say. "Why?"

"I'm getting interviewed at the Ninety-second Street Y tonight. Would you like to come along?"

"What's it about?" I ask.

"They're doing a special series about raising healthy teenagers, so it's mainly geared for parents, how to handle various problems that arise," Mom says. "I thought it would be nice to bring one of mine along."

I'm tempted to ask whether she means one of her teenagers or one of her problems. "What about Byron?"

"What about him?" Mom asks. "Can you be

ready in ten minutes? We'll grab sushi on the way."

"OK," I say, pushing aside *The Study of Matter*.

Just before Mom leaves my room, she glances at me. "Why don't you change into a dressier outfit? Some press will be there and maybe even a literary agent."

"OK."

"How about that beige sweater from Salon Z?"

"OK," I say again.

As soon as Mom is gone, I head over to my closet and pull out the beige sweater. Mom is always buying me clothes at Salon Z. That's the plus-size department of Saks Fifth Avenue. The styles aren't exactly trendy or hip. In fact, sometimes it seems like I have the wardrobe of a fifty-two-year-old woman. But Mom's good at picking out things that hide my body, so I pretty much go along with her selections.

As I yank off my sweatshirt, I think about how I don't care that Mom probably would have brought Byron to the lecture if he weren't so depressed. And I don't care that tomorrow's test on the periodic table will count for 20 percent of my chemistry grade.

I'm just happy to finally get invited to one of Mom's events.

*   *   *

Mom is going to be interviewed by a woman named Joy Lassiter. She introduces herself to me as a television journalist. She has the whitest teeth I have seen in my entire life, like a row of peppermint Chiclets.

As forty or fifty people file into the small auditorium, a cluster of us mill around near the stage. Mom is talking to a woman wearing black leather pants and a black leather jacket who introduced herself as a literary agent. Mom's face lit up when she heard that. She's always saying how she wants to write a book about being an adolescent psychologist.

A guy with a bushy ponytail sets up a video camera.

Joy Lassiter squeezes my shoulder and exclaims, "Aren't you a lucky girl!"

"Lucky?" I ask.

"To have Dr. Shreves as your mother. She really understands what it's like to be a teenager."

Mom? Mom refuses to even *talk* about her own adolescence. And as far as *my* teen years are concerned, I wouldn't exactly say Mom understands what I go through every day. But rather than telling Joy Lassiter that, I mumble, "Thanks."

As the interview begins, I settle into a chair near the front. It's impressive to see Mom in the spotlight. Joy Lassiter asks about how she became a therapist and then highlights her career accomplishments. The audience is enraptured; some people

186

are even taking notes.

When Joy starts addressing the nitty-gritty of relating to teenagers, I shift uncomfortably in my chair and attempt to follow the conversation.

Joy Lassiter: *What are the most important things for parents of teenagers to keep in mind?*

Mom: *Above all, it's important to have open and honest communication. You can't talk enough with your teenagers—even if it's hard for you, even if the subjects are controversial or taboo.*

Joy Lassiter: *How would you recommend doing all this open and honest talking?*

Mom: *What I always tell parents of my patients is that they must remember that their children aren't children anymore. They're complex, independent individuals with needs and desires that must be acknowledged and respected.*

I can't believe this. First of all, there's very little open and honest communication going on in our family. No one even says the phrase "date rape"; we just refer to it as "the ordeal." And if Mom viewed me as an independent individual whose desires must be acknowledged and respected, I'd totally be on a plane to Seattle in three days.

I feel like I can hardly breathe. I suck in some stale air, but all that makes me do is cough.

I need to get out of here.

I grab my jacket and tiptoe toward the exit. I trip over the literary agent's black leather satchel on my way, but I don't stop moving until I've hit the lobby.

It's chilly outside and the air smells like snow. I stand on the front steps, watching my breath emerge in cloudy puffs. My braces are icy against my gums, so I run my tongue over the brackets.

I walk down to East Eighty-sixth Street, where there's a bustling strip of movie theaters and restaurants. As I weave through the throngs of people, I think about how hypocritical Mom sounded back there, acting like she's this cool parent who partakes in cozy gabfests with her children.

A few summers ago, Anaïs and Mom got in a big argument. Anaïs called Mom Cleopatra, Queen of the Nile. I didn't understand why that made Mom so furious until I realized that Anaïs actually said Queen of *Denial*. As Mom stormed into her study, Anaïs shouted after her that she always brushes everything under the carpet and never deals with what's really going on.

When I think about it now, it makes sense. Like how Mom's been acting like life is normal even though Byron got kicked out of college for date rape. Or how she never talks about her childhood. Or how she always finds way to skirt around the fact that I'm heavy. It's like Mom wants our family to be perfect even when we're not.

I've always had so much respect for Mom—how she looks so together, how she has a successful career. But maybe I haven't been seeing her for who she actually is. That is, the Cleopatra part.

I don't think I've been seeing Byron for who he is either. I've spent fifteen years considering him the ideal human being. But when I stop to think about it, I remember a lot of less-than-ideal things, too. Not the date rape, but smaller incidents, things he did to me. Like when I surprised him with Rice Krispie treats up at Columbia and he acted so unwelcoming. Or how he's always making little remarks about my body. Or that day we took those photos at Grand Central Station. I'd ridden back from Connecticut with him so we could hang out that evening. But as soon as we arrived at the apartment, he got a call from a rugby buddy inviting him out that night. Before I could say *dissed and dismissed*, Byron was in the shower and out the door.

There's a guy on the corner selling hot drinks from a cart. As I reach into my pocket for some bills, I remember something Ms. Crowley told me last week.

Don't be so quick to doubt yourself, Virginia.

As I sip my hot chocolate and walk uptown

189

again, I finally understand what she meant when she said that.

Mom is standing on the front steps of the Ninety-second Street Y. She glances around to make sure no one is watching and then hisses, "Where the *fuck* were you?"

I take a few steps backward. Mom only swears when she's really upset.

"I needed some fresh air," I say.

"My interview ended twenty minutes ago. I've been standing here in the freezing cold, wondering where the hell you went." Mom's face is pinched and she's jabbing her finger in my direction. "Also, Joy announced that my teenage daughter was in the audience and asked you to stand up. She kept calling out your name. Everyone was looking around. A newspaper reporter joked about how teenagers are so unpredictable. It was mortifying."

"I'm sorry. I didn't know she was going to do that. I just—"

Mom flags down a passing cab. As it pulls up to the curb, she slides to the far end of the back seat. I get in after her and stay over on my side.

As the cab takes off, Mom starts rambling on about how she's worked so hard to get to this place in her career and how it's important to present the image of a solid family and why did I think I was entitled to chase after whatever whim came over me, especially when I should be honored that she invited me to such an important event?

I watch the traffic lights changing, the cars darting in front of each other. It's not like I'm about to tell Mom that I've realized she's a Queen of Denial who doesn't practice what she preaches.

"Don't you have anything to say?" Mom asks.

I count the different license plates within view. Three New Yorks. One New Jersey. Another New Jersey and a Connecticut.

"Say something, *dammit.*"

"OK," I finally say. "I'm going to Seattle for Thanksgiving."

"Excuse me?"

I turn to face Mom. "I'm going to Seattle for Thanksgiving."

"That's three days away! There's no way you could get a ticket at this point, even if Dad and I gave you permission."

"I already have one," I say.

"Excuse me?"

"I bought a ticket. I'm leaving on Thursday morning. I'll get back on Sunday evening. I won't miss any school. And I'll pay for the cab fare to and from the airport, so you don't have to worry about that."

"I don't give a damn about the cab fare *or* the ticket! You are *not* going to Seattle."

191

"Yes, I am."

Mom lowers her voice. "Virginia, I forbid you to go."

I take a deep breath, count to five, and say, "I'm going."

CHAPTER TWENTY-ONE

I'm on the plane to Seattle.

I can't believe this.

The pilot just announced that we might encounter turbulence. I double-check my seat belt. The flight attendant collects our trays. Today is Thanksgiving, so they served dry wedges of turkey and powdery mashed potatoes. It seemed like a strange menu since everyone will be eating the same meal tonight, but they could have given me raw Brussels sprouts and I'd still be elated.

I slept for the first leg of the trip, from New York to Denver, but I'm wide awake during this stretch. At first, I tried memorizing words from my SAT Hot 100 list. We have a huge vocabulary test the day after break. But after reading the definition of "pedantic" twelve times, I decided that I'm too wired to think about SAT words, so I put away my homework and stared out my bubble window. I watched as the plane glided over jagged expanses of the Rocky Mountains. Now we're flying over a patchwork quilt of green-and-brown earth, roads that stretch for hundreds of miles. I think it's Idaho or maybe Oregon.

The Rocky Mountains. Idaho. Oregon.

I really can't believe this.

I was convinced that I wouldn't be allowed to come. On Monday night, after I dropped the news, Mom got on the phone with the airlines, only to confirm that my ticket was nonrefundable. Then she left a frantic message on Dad's cell phone. And then she called Shannon's parents in Walla Walla. Liam and Nina must have been reassuring because Mom seemed calmer by the time she hung up.

"Well?" I asked. I was lingering in the hallway, ready to dash into my bedroom in the event of a major eruption.

"Well, *nothing.*" Mom headed into her room without saying good night.

I slept fitfully all night. The anticipation was gnawing at me. But when I woke up on Tuesday morning, Mom had already left for yoga. As I was pouring myself a bowl of cereal, Dad entered the kitchen.

"Mom and I talked last night," he said. "We've decided to let you go to Seattle."

"Daddy!" I flung my arms around his waist.

"Mom wanted me to tell you that she's still not happy with the way you handled this."

Dad was trying to look stern, but I could tell he was suppressing a grin.

Dad has been coming through a lot recently. He insisted on getting the car out of the garage to drive me to the airport this morning. He invited Mom, but she said she was too busy preparing Thanksgiving dinner. I think the real reason is that she's angry I'm going to Seattle. Mom likes to call the shots in the Shreves household, after all.

Dad and I didn't say much on the drive out of Manhattan. He listened to the weather forecast on 1010 WINS. I watched the shadowy city streets come to life. But as we hit the Triborough Bridge, Dad reached into his wallet and pulled out some twenties.

"Have fun in Seattle," he said, handing the bills to me.

I stuffed them in my backpack. "Thanks."

Dad turned down the volume on the radio. "I know it's been a difficult last few months, with everything going on with your brother. I just hope you've been OK."

I fiddled with the zipper on my bag.

Dad continued. "Our family doesn't talk about things very much. It's hard for Mom." He paused. "It's hard for all of us."

I thought about Dad's recent drinking. He's

195

curbed it a lot in the past few weeks, but this whole ordeal must be taking a toll on him, too.

"Dad?"

"Yeah?"

"Do you think maybe we could try…" I paused for a second, trying to figure out how to put it. "Do you think maybe you and I could try to communicate a little more about everything going on?"

Dad was quiet for a long time. I was about to say *forget it* when he turned to me. There were tears in the corners of his eyes.

"I would love to, Ginny," Dad said quietly. "Let's make a deal, you and me, to try to talk about things more."

I squeezed Dad's shoulder. He reached up and rested his hand on top of mine.

The pilot announces that we're beginning our descent into Seattle. We'll be landing at the Sea-Tac Airport in approximately thirty minutes. My ears feel like they're clogging up, so I yawn a few times to clear them. I tap my fingers up and down the tray table. My finger doesn't hurt anymore, but there's still a splotch on the tip that'll probably become a scar. I unwrap a piece of Trident and grind it between my teeth. I cross and uncross my legs. I continue tapping my fingers along the armrest.

I guess I'm anxious about seeing Shannon. I'm

nervous that Walla Walla has changed her, that her new friends have made her snobby or sophisticated or something. I mean, Shannon is the most grounded person in the world, but you never know what three thousand miles will do to someone.

The first thing I notice when I enter the airport is a small figure with long hair as bright as a new penny. She's waving a big, round object over her head. It looks like a softball, but as I get closer I realize it's an onion. Shannon sprints toward me, places it in my hands, and squeals, "Welcome to Washington State!"

We wrap our arms around each other and start crying.

"Did you know that some people eat a Walla Walla onion like an apple?" Shannon asks.

As I hug Shannon, my anxiety evaporates. Her hair has gotten longer and she may have gained a few freckles, but this is definitely the Shannon Iris Malloy-Newman that I know and love.

"When do we get a go at Virginia?" Nina asks.

I daub my eyes. Liam is wearing a T-shirt that says FEMINIST CHICKS DIG ME. Nina is wearing a baseball cap that says VISUALIZE WHIRLED PEAS. I have to laugh. Liam Newman and Nina Malloy are the complete opposite of my parents.

We hug and kiss and cry some more. Liam grabs my suitcase and the four of us walk, arm in arm, to the short-term parking lot. As Nina pulls onto the highway, Shannon explains that if it weren't so drizzly, we'd be able to see Mount Rainier, the nearly 15,000-foot mountain southeast of Seattle.

I clutch my onion and look out the back window. *Holy shit.* I'm in the Pacific Northwest—land of mountains rather than skyscrapers. I'm three thousand miles away from New York City, Mom, Dad, Byron, everything.

I really can't believe this.

As we approach the Claremont Hotel, Shannon bounces around in her seat.

"What?" I ask.

"My lips are sealed," she says, sliding her finger and thumb across her mouth.

"We stayed at the Claremont in August," Nina says as she switches on her left blinker. "It's in downtown Seattle. And you wouldn't believe this, Virginia, it's on—"

"Neen!" Shannon catapults through to the front seat. "Don't you remember *anything*? That's a surprise."

"*What?*" I ask again, but Shannon shoots me a mysterious look.

We pull up in front of the brick building. As Nina gives the keys to the valet and Liam checks in, Shannon steers me toward the street.

"Look where we're staying." Shannon gestures up to the sign.

198

"We're on the corner of Fourth Avenue and—"
I suck in my breath. "We're staying on Virginia
Street!"

"I know!" Shannon shrieks.

Shannon and I start singing, "We're staying on
Virginia Street! We're staying on Virginia Street!"
I bought a disposable camera in the Denver airport, so I pull it out of my backpack and Shannon
gets a few shots of me standing under the street
sign.

Liam summons us into the lobby. "Rules for
Seattle," he says, handing Shannon our room key.
"Stick together all the time. I know you girls run
around Manhattan, but we're talking about an
entirely new city. Rule number two. Make sure
you have a cup of coffee every day. Even if you
don't like coffee, you'll love it here. And lastly,
paint the town red by daylight, but meet us in the
lobby every night at six."

"Are we excused?" Shannon asks, rolling her
eyes.

Liam swats her with a Seattle guidebook.
"You're excused."

Our room is small but elegant, with antique
cherry furniture, two double beds, plush white
bathrobes, and a collection of miniature Neutrogena products. Shannon and I flop onto one of the
beds and talk for over an hour. Around five-thirty,
Shannon pulls out a tube of silver glitter and we

roll streaks onto our temples and cheeks. As I brush my hair, Shannon braids hers into pigtails. We decide not to change our clothes because Nina said the dress code in Seattle is casual with a capital C.

When we arrive in the lobby, Liam and Nina are sitting on a couch in front of the fireplace. Liam is reading the *Seattle Post-Intelligencer*. Nina is reading a manuscript. She's a freelance copyeditor, so she's always buried in a stack of papers. Shannon is the physical clone of Nina, down to the red hair and the Milky Way of freckles, but when it comes to energy level, she's totally her dad.

"The glitter girls!" Liam gives us both a hug. "Do either of you feel like turkey? Because although Nina and I are having major Thanksgiving guilt, we're craving Asian food."

"How unpatriotic," Shannon says, wryly.

Liam turns to me. "Virginia, do you have any thoughts on the matter?"

I shrug. "Anything's fine with me."

"Not good enough," Liam says. "We need an opinion. We need to be swayed."

"I had turkey on the airplane," I say.

"Then it's settled!" Liam claps his hands together. "Neen! Put down that manuscript. We're having Thai food tonight."

We drive up to a neighborhood called Capitol Hill. It reminds me of the East Village, with ethnic restaurants and tattooed twenty-somethings milling about. Liam leads us to a Thai place, where we devour a vegetarian meal and declare it our best Thanksgiving dinner ever. I can't help but think about the traditional Thanksgiving that took place on Riverside Drive tonight—turkey and stuffing and Mom rambling on about how she's thankful for a *wooonderful* family and *wooonderful* friends and a *wooonderful* life.

After dinner we wander down Broadway, which is the main street running through Capitol Hill. Liam and Nina are holding hands and reading dessert menus at various cafés. As Shannon and I trail behind, we tally up the various bodily locations where we've seen piercings this evening. So far, it's cheeks, eyebrows, lips, ears, chins, tongues, and one shirtless guy with a ring through his nipple. We're just musing about below-the-waist possibilities when we stumble upon an arrangement of small bronze footprints embedded into the sidewalk. Upon closer inspection, we realize they're marking the steps for the rumba. Shannon and I start following the numbered footprints, doing the rumba. As soon as Liam and Nina spot us, they join in and the four of us dance until we're laughing so hard that our stomachs cramp up.

When we get back to the hotel, Shannon and I scrub our faces with the tiny bar of Neutrogena. She strips down right in front of me, pulling a

T-shirt over her head. I head into the bathroom to change into my flannel pajamas, but Shannon doesn't make me feel self-conscious about the fact that I prefer to undress in private.

We decide to share one of the double beds. Shannon pulls back the covers. I crawl in after her and slide over, so we're lying shoulder to shoulder.

As soon as Shannon switches off the light, she says, "Do you want to play Fairy Godmother?"

"Sure."

We always used to play Fairy Godmother during sleepovers in junior high. The game goes like this: If you had a fairy godmother who could wave a magic wand over your head and grant you three wishes, what would you ask for? The only rule of Fairy Godmother is that you have to be completely honest.

"You start," Shannon says.

"My first wish is easy. I wish I were thin. I wish I had the perfect body."

"Kazam," Shannon says, tapping my forehead with her finger. "And your second wish?"

"I want a boyfriend who loves me and accepts me and we're great friends and he has a sense of humor and he's totally hot. And please, Fairy God-mother," I add, "if you decide to make him have green eyes and play shortstop for the Yankees, I wouldn't have a problem with it."

Shannon giggles as she pats my forehead. "One

ball-playing boyfriend, coming right up."

"For my third wish…" I let that thought trail off. Shannon and I haven't talked about my brother at all since I arrived. I've been enjoying the vacation from all the drama in New York. It's a relief not to have it occupying my brain every single second. Even so, the rules of Fairy Godmother are strict. You must be honest about your wishes.

"I wish this whole ordeal with Byron never happened," I say quickly. "I wish it would disappear and we could go back to the way things used to be."

When Shannon reaches over, I assume she's going to touch my forehead, but she slides her arm under the covers and squeezes my hand.

"Before I grant that wish I want you to say it out loud. I've never heard you say it out loud."

"Say what?"

"What your brother did."

I turn to face Shannon. The room is dark, so I can only see the silhouette of her profile. Could she possibly be right? I've been obsessing about the date rape so much these past six weeks, but I don't think I've ever actually said those two words out loud. I guess we've all just followed Mom's lead and called it "the ordeal" or "why Byron got suspended from Columbia."

"OK." I take a shallow breath. "Rape. Date rape."

"Who? What?"

"Byron. Byron date-raped a girl. No, not a girl. Annie Mills. Byron date-raped Annie Mills."

"And you wish it never happened?"

"Yeah. I mean, shouldn't I?"

"Of course you should wish he never did it." Shannon pauses before adding, "But he did."

I'm quiet for a long time. I think about that quote Shannon read me from the tea box, about how everything in life is tied together, that nothing stands by itself. She shared it with me the morning after I found out about the date rape so I was like, *What on earth are you talking about?* But now it hits me how much I've learned about Byron since then. I mean, it's not like he's done to me what he did to Annie Mills, but he hasn't exactly been the perfect big brother these past few years. And I probably wouldn't have even realized that if it hadn't been for this big-time wake-up call.

"Did you ever think Byron could do something like this?" I ask.

"I never considered date rape," Shannon says. "But I can't say I thought he walked on water, like you did. Maybe it's different because he's not my brother, but I'd hear the things he'd say to you or watch the way he'd blow you out all the time."

"I know, Shan. I've been thinking about that so much recently." I choke up, making it hard to talk. "It's just … I don't know … it's just confusing to see this all so clearly for the first time."

204

I'm really crying by this point. My nose is running and my stomach is heaving. Shannon wraps her arms around me.

"I've missed you, Virginia," Shannon whispers.

"I've missed you, too," I say, wiping my wet cheeks on the sheet. "More than you can imagine."

CHAPTER TWENTY-TWO

It's Saturday afternoon. Shannon and I are sitting on a pier sipping hazelnut lattés and watching ferries shuttle to Bainbridge Island. Over the past two days, we've done everything under the sun. Or I guess I should say rain. It rains constantly in Seattle. The hotel loaned us a huge black umbrella and, fueled on various coffee concoctions, we explored Pike Place Market—an open-air market on the waterfront where fish vendors fling salmon through the air. We trekked back up to Capitol Hill. We even had Liam and Nina drive us past Bill Gates's $100 million-dollar mansion.

I took a picture of it for Froggy in case he ever talks to me again. It's been over a month since the incident at my locker, and he still hasn't said a word to me. Shannon thinks he's probably licking his wounds, that guys have sensitive egos that way.

I'm convinced that Froggy was legally blind in September but sold his trombone so he could get laser surgery on his eyes. Now that he can see what I actually look like, he can't believe he ever came near me.

Yesterday Shannon and I rode an elevator to the top of this futuristic tower called the Space Needle. The skies were clear, so we got a stunning view of Puget Sound, the Cascade Mountains, and the Olympic Mountains. Looking south, I was blown away by Mount Rainier. It's the tallest, widest mountain I could ever imagine, just like those snowcapped peaks I drew when I was a kid. As I gaped at Mount Rainier, I was both speechless and elated.

That's how I've been since I arrived in Seattle. Not speechless as much as elated. For the first time in months, I've been laughing at even the silliest things. I'm not distracted all the time. And being around Shannon, who rarely talks to strangers for fear of stuttering, makes me more outgoing. I've been babbling to every person on the street, asking for directions or striking up random conversations. The strangest thing is that I'm not thinking about food all the time. Rather than constantly munching, like I do at home, I'm just eating when I'm hungry. I'm not back on my diet, but I may have lost a few pounds because my Fat Pants are feeling a little loose.

Shannon and I have decided we want to do something special to commemorate this weekend. That's what we're discussing now, down at the pier.

"Friendship rings?" Shannon suggests.

"Too overdone."

"Toe rings?"

"My toes are really sensitive," I say. "It would drive me crazy."

I hear a foghorn blaring in the distance. A guy wearing combat boots passes our bench. He's got a shaved head, dozens of studs in his ears, and a ring through his nostril.

"Hey, you!" I shout to him.

I don't know who looks more surprised, the guy or Shannon. He freezes in his tracks and stares at me.

"Where do you get body piercing done around here?" I ask.

Shannon grabs hold of my hand and squeals.

"Lots of places." He scratches his bare head. "How old are you?"

"Seventeen," I lie.

Shannon digs her fingernails into my palm.

"Unless your parents come along, most places won't pierce you until you're eighteen."

Shannon and I must look devastated because the guy sits down on the bench with us. Shannon adjusts the umbrella, so it's covering him as well.

"I know a guy named Sage at a place on Capitol Hill," he says. "It's called Holy Moly. He's the one with the lime-green Mohawk. If you tell him I sent you, he'll hook you up."

"What's your name?" I ask.

"X," he says.

"X?" Shannon and I ask in unison.

The guy smiles sheepishly. "My real name is Matthew, but don't tell Sage that."

Shannon and I walk to the corner, where we hop on an electric bus that's attached to overhead cables. On the ride to Capitol Hill, we discuss the factors of a potential piercing.

There's the legal issue, but we both agree that we won't be deterred by age limits. It's not like they can send someone to jail for getting a nose ring.

Then there's the parental factor.

"Liam and Nina will love it. They're always saying they want matching bellybutton rings." Shannon gives me a sympathetic look. "What about yours?"

"They'll hate it," I say. "But they can't exactly make me live in a refrigerator box, so what's the worst that can happen?"

Then we discuss the most pressing element—bodily location. I've decided to get an eyebrow ring. I want something on my face, but nose rings are too gross, what with the booger factor. Chin studs look like zits. And I'm worried a lip ring would get torn out by my braces.

"What about you?" I ask.

Shannon stares out the bus window. "My tongue," she says quietly.

"You're getting your *tongue* pierced?"

Shannon nods. "I've spent my entire life hating my tongue because it makes me stutter. It's time to start bonding with it."

We find Holy Moly right away. Sage, the only person in the shop with a lime-green Mohawk, is discussing aftercare with a woman who has just gotten a stud through her cheek. We linger around the counter for a few minutes, admiring tattoo templates. When Sage finally comes over, we explain our situation and tell him that X thought he could help us.

"For X," Sage says, "I'll do anything."

Sage starts by examining what he calls "the webbing" on Shannon's tongue, which he proceeds to deem pierceable. Then, as he reviews prices and procedures, I count my money. With the cash from Dad, I've got enough for the eyebrow ring. Sage writes down our names and tells us to return in a half-hour.

We walk over to Broadway and grab some pepperoni pizza. Sage recommended that Shannon eat a fortifying meal since she might not be able to deal with solid foods for a few days after the piercing.

 210

Once we're done, we wander into a funky vintage shop. Shannon buys a plastic ring. I buy a polyester orange shirt with horizontal green stripes. Mom's always telling me I should stick to neutral colors. And definitely no horizontal stripes, since they reveal extra poundage. But something about the shirt beckons me. Besides, it's only five bucks so I can always toss it if I change my mind.

On our way back to Holy Moly, Shannon asks, "You sure you want to do this?"

"Surer than ever."

Twenty minutes later, I have a silver ring in my left eyebrow and Shannon has a stainless steel barbell through her tongue. The pain wasn't bad, at least for me. Sage fastened on clamps to hold the skin in place and told me to take a deep breath. It felt like a sharp pinch when the needle went through. I definitely flinched, but it was over pretty quickly.

Shannon went next. As Sage marked a dot on her tongue, she was trembling like a dog during a thunderstorm. I didn't blame her for being anxious because although Sage reassured her that he was quite experienced, he *did* explain that there are risks involved when piercing a tongue, like hitting a vein. It hurt so badly that Shannon teared up. I held her hand as she winced in pain. Sage said it'll be healed in no time, like six weeks, so she took some comfort in that.

Then he launched into a lecture about cleaning and maintenance. I promised him I would be scrupulously sterile, but even so he warned me that it'll take three months to heal.

I don't care if it takes three years because I love my eyebrow ring. I loved it the second Sage held up the mirror so I could see the new addition to my face.

"I can't believe it," I kept repeating as I stared at my reflection.

It was like I was seeing myself for the very first time.

"Here's to facial ornamentation!" Liam raises a glass of water in the air.

"Here, here." I clink with him.

"Heee, heee," Shannon says. It's hard for her to talk with a swollen tongue.

Nina sips her beer. "Will you please tell your parents we had nothing to do with this?"

I dip a piece of bread into olive oil. "I'll take all the blame."

"Tell them we're furious with Shannon," Liam says as he studies the menu.

We're eating at a restaurant called the Pink Door. It's on Post Alley, which is walking distance from the Claremont. There's no sign outside, so you just have to look for the pink door.

While we're waiting for the waitress to come

over, I tell them the story of Sage and X. Shannon nods and makes guttural noises.

"After I've finished my book on onions," Liam says, "I'm thinking of proposing a book about people with unusual names."

I consider mentioning Froggy Welsh the Fourth, but then the waitress arrives to take our order.

After dinner we head right back to the hotel. My flight leaves at eight-thirty tomorrow morning, so Nina is giving us a wake-up call at five-thirty. They're going to drive me to the airport and then continue on to Walla Walla. Nina makes both of us take Advil before we go to our room, in case the pain increases overnight.

Shannon switches on the television and starts sucking an ice cube. I go into the bathroom and turn on the shower. I glance into the mirror. I can't believe how much I love my eyebrow ring. It makes me look unique and interesting. I stare at my reflection for about five minutes, checking out my face from every possible angle.

I step into the shower. It's the kind that has a detachable nozzle. As I run the nozzle over my chest, I think about Froggy. I've been thinking about him a lot since I've been in Seattle. Whenever I do, I get this pang in my stomach. I wish I could make things better. I miss kissing him, but I also just miss the way I felt in his presence—sort of giggly and girlish.

213

I probably shouldn't have denounced everything having to do with the opposite sex. What Byron did was horrible, but I have to remember that that was date rape. And forcing yourself onto someone is *completely* different than consensual fooling around, which is what Froggy and I were doing. I think I got them jumbled together in my head.

I lower the nozzle so it sprays a stream of warm water between my legs. This is the first time I've touched myself like this in months. I don't hold the nozzle there for long, just enough to send a tingling sensation through my body.

That's when it dawns on me.

At some point over the past few days, I've stopped feeling numb.

CHAPTER TWENTY-THREE

Mom and Dad are waiting for me at the airport. I think they're even smiling. Liam and Nina overnighted them fresh salmon packed on ice, so maybe that cushioned the blow of my running away to Seattle.

As I get closer, Mom's smile fades. "What's on your face?"

My hand wanders to my eyebrow. I'm about to touch the ring when I remember that Sage told me not to fiddle with it. "An eyebrow ring."

"I know what it is. But what is it doing on *your* eyebrow?"

"I like it," Dad says.

"Don't encourage her, Mike."

Dad reaches for my suitcase.

"Let's go," Mom says. "We'll discuss it later."

None of us talk much on the ride home. Mom

says they appreciated the salmon from Liam and Nina. Dad asks if I went up in the Space Needle. I tell them that we stayed on Virginia Street. Dad says he bought capers to eat with the salmon. Mom asks when the Space Needle was built. I repeat that we stayed on Virginia Street.

As soon as we get back to the apartment, Mom grabs a book and disappears into their bedroom. Dad joins Byron on the couch, where he's watching a Knicks game. I go into the kitchen and devour two slices of leftover pumpkin pie drenched in homemade whipped cream.

As I'm heading into my bedroom, Byron calls out, "Welcome home, Gin."

"Thanks."

In the old days, I would have paraded over and shown him my eyebrow ring. If he liked it, I would have been the happiest person on the planet. If he said it looked dumb, I would have taken it out instantly. But now I couldn't care less what Byron thinks.

I'm on my way into school the next morning when I run into Ms. Crowley.

"A true Seattle babe!" she exclaims, admiring my eyebrow ring.

I give her the quick scoop on my trip, promising to fill her in at lunch.

As soon as the bell rings, I scurry up to global

studies. We're midway through the terrorism unit. Mr. Vandenhausler spends the first several minutes explaining how the best way to trap terrorists is to get inside their heads, to understand the nuts and bolts of their operations. His mustache twitches like a rattlesnake's tail as he instructs us to break into small groups and pretend that we are masterminding a terrorist attack.

I wind up in a group with Alyssa Wu and three guys. The guys are debating whether to hijack an airplane or go the biological-warfare route. Alyssa is knitting. She must have noticed me watching her because she leans toward me and whispers, "I love your eyebrow ring."

"Thanks."

"Did you get it done downtown?"

"No, it was at a place in Seattle. That's where I went over Thanksgiving."

"Lucky," she says. "All I did was go to Delaware where my family fought for four days and my dad was only thankful that he wasn't the turkey."

I crack up.

"Alyssa Wu! Virginia Shreves!" Mr. Vandenhausler marches over to our desks. "Terrorism is not a laughing matter. Do you think the FBI and the CIA are giggling right now? As a matter of fact—" Mr. Vandenhausler stops when he notices my eyebrow ring. "Virginia, when did you get your eyebrow pierced?"

"Over Thanksgiving break."

Mr. Vandenhausler's mustache twitches ever so slightly. "Did it hurt?"

I nod.

"Serious pain?" he asks.

"Not that bad."

Mr. Vandenhausler looks disappointed. "Well, get back to terrorism, girls. You've got a world to save."

That's how it's been all day. People who I never thought noticed me before have been telling me how great my eyebrow ring looks. It's funny. I always assumed an Iron Rule of the High School Way of Life is that only the cool crowd is allowed to take fashion risks and if a regular/dorky person does something wacky, then everyone will call them a poseur or a wannabe. But the strangest thing is that that hasn't been happening at all.

Even Brie Newhart notices my eyebrow ring. We're sitting in French, waiting for class to begin. I can tell she's staring at my eyebrow, so I turn and smile at her.

"I want to get my nose pierced," she says, "but I'm scared of needles."

"It wasn't that bad. It took under thirty seconds."

"Really? That's all?"

I nod.

If someone told me a few months ago that Brie

218

and I would have a normal humanly exchange, I would have been like, *Yeah, right*. But I'm not so floored now. I guess I'm feeling a little different about things, like how outside appearances can be deceiving and sometimes people aren't all they're cracked up to be. Speaking of appearances, Brie looks pale and worn out, like a T-shirt that's been in the dryer too many times. She's not quite as intimidating as she was back in September.

Mademoiselle Kiefer claps her hands together. I glance at Froggy. He got a haircut over break, reducing his cowlick to a little ridge on his forehead.

If only Froggy would notice my eyebrow ring. Now *that* would make my day.

It's the second to last day in November. I just got home from school. I'm in my bathroom cleaning my eyebrow. I've been following the aftercare instructions to the letter. I start by removing crusty matter around the pierce hole. There's not a lot, just a few flakes of skin. I dip a Q-Tip into warm water, wet down the area, and apply a smidgen of Dial.

The door to the bathroom is cracked open. No one's home, so I have Z100 pumped in my room. I'm singing along with the radio as I lather the antibacterial soap.

Mom peeks into the bathroom.

I stop singing. "What are you doing home?"

"I have to pick up some files," she says. "Can you talk for a minute?"

I continue soaping my eyebrow. Z100 has just announced that they're doing an hour-long tribute to women hip-hop singers.

Mom sits down on the toilet lid and takes a ShrinkBreath—in through the nose and out through the mouth. "I've been thinking a lot about your recent rebellions," she says. "Buying that ticket to Seattle and now this." Mom gestures in the direction of my face.

Ashanti starts singing "Foolish." It's on loudly, so Mom has to raise her voice to be audible.

"I realize that the teen years are a time to assert your autonomy, to establish an identity separate from your family. Anaïs went through this stage, just a few years later." Mom takes another ShrinkBreath. "I just want you to think carefully about your actions. I don't like to see you being so impetuous."

"Impetuous" is on my SAT Hot 100 list. It means "sudden and spontaneous," which is *exactly* what I'd like to be. I decide not to inform Mom of that. Instead, I lean over the faucet and rinse my eyebrow.

"Having a ring through your eyebrow seems so barbaric," Mom says. "I can hardly look at it without wincing."

 220

Ashanti is singing about how she keeps running back to someone even though he treats her badly. I carefully slide the ring back and forth to make sure the pierce is clean.

"When women first started getting their ears pierced, everyone thought *that* was barbaric," I say. "But now it's as normal as necklaces. I think it's the same with facial piercings. It'll just take time to get used to them."

"The two aren't comparable, Virginia. Piercing your ears is easy and relatively painless. Getting a hole through your eyebrow ... that's just, well, unattractive. You looked much better without it."

"In your opinion," I say. "Besides, my eyebrow was easy and relatively painless, too."

Mom clenches her jaw. "Look, I just wanted to say that I'd like you to—"

I cut her off. "If you're trying to convince me to take out my eyebrow ring, I'm sorry. It's here to stay."

Mom stands up so quickly that a towel hanging on the shower rack slips to the floor. "I don't know what's gotten into you, but I don't like it."

As she marches out of the bathroom, I pat my eyebrow with a cotton ball.

"I'll tell you what's gotten into me," I call after her. "I'm finally having a little fun in my life."

But Ashanti has launched into a chorus of "*never gonna change*," so I don't think Mom hears me.

One of the side effects of not being numb anymore is that I'm starting to realize what I want and I'm sticking to it. Which pisses the hell out of Mom.

I'm dreading our shopping trip today.

It's been over a week since the bathroom showdown, and Mom and I are still on pins and needles. We haven't had a blowout, though we've been making a lot of snippy comments back and forth. But the Lowensteins' annual holiday party is less than two weeks away, and Mom is insisting that I get something new to wear and that it come from Saks. I know what that means. Salon Z. The plus-size floor.

It's Sunday afternoon. Dad and Byron are at a Knicks game. Mom and I are riding the elevator downstairs.

"Why can't we go to Strawberry?" I ask. Strawberry is a funky discount store that I've browsed in before, but I've never had the guts to buy anything there. I like that they have cool clothes in every size, from extra-small to extra-large. And they're all mixed together, so the fat girls aren't banished to the fat floor where the dresses look like gunnysacks and the mannequins resemble embalmed grandmothers.

"Strawberry?" Mom scrunches her nose. "It's so cheap-looking. We're going to a holiday party, not the Jersey Shore."

 222

"What about Old Navy?"

"Too casual," Mom says.

We step onto Riverside Drive. There's a bitter wind whipping in from the river. The doorman flags a cab. Mom tells the driver to take us to Saks.

Saks is swamped with holiday shoppers. We weave our way to the elevator bank. Mom presses the button for the tenth floor. Salon Zit. Salon Zero. Salon Zaftig.

"Mom?"

"Yes?"

"Maybe we can check out the teen section instead?"

"But..." Mom glances uncomfortably at the other shoppers in the elevator.

I press the button for the fifth floor. I'm not sure what's come over me. I guess I just want to wear something more fun for my holiday outfit this year. More colors. More curves. Maybe even a little flesh exposure.

When the elevator arrives on the fifth floor, I head into the teen section. Mom hesitantly follows.

The only way to compare the teen styles to the Salon Z styles is likening it to West Berlin and East Berlin before the wall came down. Completely different universes only an arm's length apart.

"Do you really think we'll find something flattering for you?" Mom asks as I eye a stretchy black dress with sequins around the chest. "I mean, these aren't exactly…"

"You never know," I say, plunking the black dress off the rack.

I gaze at a row of sparkly red velvet gowns. They're really glamorous, like something a movie star might wear to the Academy Awards.

"I don't know, Virginia," Mom says. "Red isn't really your color. Why don't we find something a little less attention-grabbing?"

"I like red," I say, taking the gown in two different sizes.

Mom digs a Certs out of her purse and pops it into her mouth.

I'm just checking out some silky kimono-style dresses when Mom holds up a pale green satin number. It's very roomy. And very pale green.

"What do you think?" she asks.

"It looks like a bridesmaid dress," I say.

Mom grinds the Certs between her teeth so loudly I can hear it three racks away. "You don't have to try it on."

"No, I will."

Once we've selected five dresses, we follow signs to the dressing room. It has an abundance of mirrors, which are thankfully *outside* the stalls. They're piping an orchestral version of "Silent Night" over the sound system. I settle into a stall and strip down to my undies and socks.

224

I can hear Mom pacing nervously outside my door. I try on the black sequined dress. Even though it's stretchy, I can barely tug it over my hips. I wriggle out of it, toss it on the little bench, and move on to the largest of the red velvet gowns.

"So?" Mom asks.

"Still trying."

The red gown is too snug. So are the kimonos. The only one that actually fits is Mom's pale-green selection. And even with that one, I can only zip it halfway up my back.

I glance down at myself. I look like an overgrown avocado.

"Any luck?" Mom asks. I hear another Certs crunch in her mouth.

"None are quite right."

"What's wrong?"

"They don't exactly fit."

I hear the saleswoman suggesting we check out Salon Z.

"Honey," Mom says, "let's go up to Salon Z. That's where we should have started in the first place. We can look for something a little more layered."

"I don't want to go to Salon Z," I say, sitting on the bench and folding my arms across my chest. I sound like a brat, but I don't care. I mean, do I have to write it in blood? I. Do. Not. Want. To. Wear. Any. More. Ugly. Clothes. From. Salon. Z.

"Why not?" Mom asks. There's an edge in her voice, like she's losing her patience.

"Because the clothes make me look like a dumpy old great-aunt."

Mom takes a few steps closer to my stall, so she's right against the door. "With your body type, Virginia," she whispers, "it's better to go for layers. I should know."

"Salon Z has a lot of attractive plus-size clothing," the saleswoman chimes in. "You'd be surprised at the…"

"What body type are you talking about?" I ask, standing up. I'm on the verge of tears.

"We'll talk about this later," Mom says in a hiss-whisper.

I fling open the door, even though I'm half squeezed into the avocado dress. "Why can't you say it out loud, Mom?" I shout. "I'm fat, OK? F-A-T. But that doesn't mean I have to hide beneath layers of fabric. That doesn't mean I'm exactly like you used to be, ashamed of showing my body. That doesn't mean I have to get my dress from stupid old Salo—"

Mom cuts me off. "I've had quite enough of you this afternoon," she says curtly.

I slam the door and start crying. My face is hot and my nose is streaming.

"Meet me at the elevators as soon as you've changed," Mom says through the door. "We're going home."

Mom's footsteps recede from the dressing room.

I kick the wall of my stall. It leaves a small indentation. I kick it again, harder this time. I'm only wearing socks, so I bash my toes pretty badly, sending a jarring shock through my whole body.

As the orchestral "Silent Night" hits the sleep-in-heavenly-peace part, I collapse to the floor and sob for five minutes straight.

Chapter Twenty-Four

I think the second toe on my right foot is broken. It hurts so badly that I can't put any weight on that foot without shrieking. When I e-mailed Shannon about it, she instructed me to go to the emergency room immediately. But Dad left for a business trip yesterday evening, and Mom is so angry that if I asked her for anything, she'd probably go after my nine intact toes.

On Monday morning I hobble to school and wince my way through first period. When I arrive in gym, Teri takes one look at me and sends me to the nurse's office. Paul hands me an ice pack and tries my parents' office and cell phones. He can't reach Dad and Mom is with patients all morning, so her secretary gives him the number for my doctor.

Dr. Love's office says they can fit me in right

away. I give Paul my locker combination. He retrieves my jacket and backpack, helps me outside, and loans me cab money.

Now that I know this can get me out of school so easily, I'll have to make a career out of breaking my toes.

That's a joke.

Sort of.

As soon as Dr. Love enters the examination room, he compliments my eyebrow ring.

"How's it healing?"

"Pretty well," I say. "It doesn't hurt that much."

"Mind if I take a look?"

"Go ahead."

Dr. Love washes his hands. As he approaches the table, I pull aside my eyebrow ring so he can get a better look at the pierce.

"What happened to your finger?" Dr. Love asks.

I lower my hand to my side. "I burned myself."

"How?"

"Truth?"

Dr. Love nods.

"On a candle."

As he examines my finger, his face looks concerned. "You should rub vitamin E oil on it every night. That'll reduce scarring." Dr. Love checks out my eyebrow ring and then sits on his rotating stool. "So what's up with your toe?"

"I think it's broken."

"How did it happen?"

"I was pissed at my mom so I kicked a wall in Saks."

"If you've got to kick somewhere," Dr. Love says, laughing.

I crack up, too.

He gingerly unlaces my sneaker and rolls off my sock. After examining my toe, he says that while he's almost certain it's broken, he's not going to send me for x-rays because either way he'll just have to tape it up.

"Speaking of your mom," Dr. Love says as he tapes my wounded toe to my third toe, "I owe you an apology."

"Me? Why?"

"When you were here for your last visit, I regretted involving her in that discussion. Weight is such a dicey issue, especially for mothers and daughters. I firmly believe that it's about feeling good, regardless of your body type. I'm not sure your mom understands that."

I choke up. I can't believe what a relief it is to hear this out loud, like I'm not a factory defect or something.

Dr. Love hands me a tissue. "Going through a hard time with your family right now?"

I nod.

230

"I bet you're pretty angry."

I blow my nose.

"Anger is a healthy emotion," Dr. Love says, "as long as you can find ways to channel it where you don't hurt yourself in the process."

I glance at my burnt finger, my broken toe.

"Have you ever tried kickboxing?" Dr. Love asks.

I wipe my eyes. "Is it like aerobics? Because that's really not my thing."

"No, it's nothing like aerobics. Kickboxing combines traditional martial arts with boxing, stretching, and breathing techniques. A friend of mine teaches a class geared for teenage girls." Dr. Love pulls out his prescription pad and jots down the name and address of the gym. "It's a great way to release anger, not to mention build strength and flexibility."

"It sounds interesting," I say.

"Give your toe a few weeks to heal and then check it out."

By the time I leave Dr. Love's office, the temperature has plummeted. My toe feels a little better now that it's taped up. I zip my jacket and limp toward the subway station.

That's when it hits me. I'm three blocks from Columbia. I haven't been to Columbia since late September, when I surprised Byron in his dorm room.

231

My heart is pounding as I reach the main entranceway to the campus. I stare up at the imposing gate, topped with golden crowns and flanked by toga-wearing statues.

Somewhere inside of there, Annie Mills is living, breathing, suffering.

I shuffle through the gate and nimbly navigate the brick pathways, which are slick with ice. It's hard to imagine that Annie Mills is a real person. No one in my family ever talks about her, so she exists only in my imagination, a tragic figure whose life was destroyed by my brother.

My heart is punching against my chest as I stop a woman on the path and ask where I can find a student directory. She points me toward a glass building and tells me to look for the computers near the café.

By the time I make it into the building, my ears are frostbitten and my neck is stinging. I thaw out for a second before heading to a computer. I click the box on the screen labeled "student directory" and enter A-n-n-i-e M-i-l-l-s.

It pops up on the screen, just like that.

Her phone number and room and everything. My knees are buckling. Annie Mills lives in Wallach, the same dorm as Byron. I glance nervously over my shoulder before scribbling the information onto the back of the paper from Dr. Love. Then I close the screen, grab my backpack, and hobble off campus.

As soon as I get home, I put the prescription paper in my cedar box, strip down to my T-shirt, and crawl into bed, where I remain for the rest of the day.

CHAPTER TWENTY-FIVE

My toe has healed steadily over the past ten days. Even so, I've been excused from gym. Brie Newhart has been complaining of dizzy spells, so Teri won't let her participate either. Some mornings we set up cones or inflate volleyballs, but usually we just do our homework together.

Brie has been helping me understand the difference between a relative pronoun and an object pronoun in French. And I have a better grasp on the books we've been reading for "Ostracism and Oppression," so I give her pointers for her language arts papers. It's not like we chat much, but I think we've established a silent peace treaty. At least I have. I'm not so obsessed with what she said about me in the bathroom anymore. I mean, I've heard her puking in that same stall three times now, so I hardly think she's in a position to judge *me*.

Mostly, I just appreciate her help with my French homework.

I'm really suffering in French. I may get my first C ever. My mind wanders so much during class. I can't stop looking over at Froggy. I've spotted him walking out of school with Sarah, the freshman girl with the ski-jump nose. Seeing that she's most likely Froggy's girlfriend, I shouldn't spend French class pining after him. But I just can't help it.

I wish I could memorize French pronouns the way I've memorized Annie Mills's contact information. I take the paper out of my cedar box all the time just to look at it, to think about how Byron once called that number, maybe even visited that room.

Speaking of Byron, he's in a good mood today. It's Wednesday afternoon, a week before Christmas. I'm watching *Total Request Live* and munching on chocolate-covered pretzels when the buzzer rings.

Byron jogs into the foyer, humming a song that was just on *TRL*.

"Who's here?" I ask.

"Some friends called earlier to see if they could swing by."

It turns out to be that guy I met in Byron's dorm, the one who looks like a hamster. He's holding hands with an Indian woman wearing a knee-length skirt and tall black boots. Byron offers to get them something to drink, but Hamster Boy coolly explains that he just stopped by to get those DVDs he loaned my brother last fall.

They're in and out in less than five minutes, not enough time for the slush from their boots to melt into puddles.

As soon as they're gone, Byron knocks around the kitchen, clanking dishes and slamming cupboards.

"Could you keep it down?" I grab the remote and pump the volume on MTV.

"Get off my back," Byron barks from the kitchen.

"What's gotten into you?"

"Why do *you* care?"

"I care because you're interrupting *TRL*," I shout. They're about to announce the top video of the day and I don't want to miss it.

"Fine." Byron stomps into the living room. "I was interested in that girl and Shawn, the little prick, chased after her as soon as I was out of sight."

Before I can stop myself, I say, "Well it's not like anyone will want to go out with you anymore."

"What are you talking about?"

"You know what I'm talking about." I give him a knowing look. "Annie Mills."

Byron pales. "Don't go there, Gin."

"Why not?"

"Because it's none of your fucking business."

"Maybe it's none of my fucking business," I say, "but I'm just saying that I'm probably not the only person who thinks you're an asshole for date-raping someone."

Byron lurches toward me. I tumble over the back of the couch, truck into my bedroom, and turn the lock.

Byron pounds on my door. "Come out, you fat piece of shit!"

"Fuck you!" I shout. I'm trembling all over.

"No, fuck *you*!"

Byron goes into his bedroom and blasts his music. I dig that photo strip of us out of my cedar box, tear it to shreds, and chuck it into my trash. I'm looking around my room for other remnants of my brother when I spot a paper clip on my desk. I'm tempted to unbend the wire and run it across my wrist until I break the skin. I can picture the dots of blood oozing to the surface, releasing the anger inside my chest.

That's when I remember what Dr. Love said about not hurting myself anymore. Instead, I grab my jacket and hurry out of the apartment before Byron hears me and pummels me to a pulp.

I take the subway up Broadway and walk across Columbia's main campus. The sky is hazy and snowflakes litter the air. They're forecasting a blizzard this evening, four to six inches of snow-fall.

I find Wallach right away, but I have to wait on the front stoop for nearly twenty minutes, shivering and rubbing my hands together, until enough students are crowded into the entranceway for me to slip past the security guard.

Annie Mills's room is 209, so I take the narrow stairs to the second floor. I make my way down several hallways, past the 230s and the 220s. As I get closer, my heart is beating so hard it feels like it's going to crack my ribs.

Room 212 … 211 … 210…

There it is. Room 209.

I raise my hand and knock on the door.

"Who is it?" a voice calls from inside.

Is that Annie Mills? Or maybe her roommate?

I knock again.

I can hear footsteps crossing the room. The woman who opens the door has amber-colored eyes and tangly brown hair that reaches her waist. She's wearing an off-white undershirt, overalls, and no makeup.

"May I help you?" she asks.

"Are you Annie Mills?"

"Yeah."

"I'm Virginia Shreves. My older brother is By—"

"Byron Shreves." Annie frowns. "What are you doing here?"

 238

I chew on a fingernail, even though it's already ground down to the skin. I prepared what I was going to say on the subway, but now my mind is blank.

Annie twists a long strand of hair around her finger. "I'm not exactly sure you should be..."

"You're right." I choke up. "I'm sorry ... it was a stupid idea."

I turn and take off. Once I reach the stairwell, I plunk down on the top step. I'm shaking all over—from nerves, but also from being cold. My hair is damp and my sneakers are soggy and freezing. I can't believe I'm sniffling and shivering in a dingy stairwell of a dorm.

That's when it hits me. I came to Columbia for a reason. Partially, I needed to see Annie, to confirm that she's a real person. But I also wanted to apologize to her. I know I'm not responsible for Byron's actions, but she deserves to have some sympathy from one Shreves.

I stand up, take a few deep breaths, and head back toward room 209. When I reach her door, I wipe my eyes and nose, take a calming breath, and knock.

The door opens right away.

"Hey," I say.

Annie looks confused.

"I'm sorry to bother you." I stare down at my wet sneakers, willing myself not to cry. "I just wanted to say I'm sorry for what my brother did to you. If it makes any difference, I think he's an asshole for wrecking your life like that."

Annie doesn't respond, so I quickly add, "Well, that's all. I guess I'll head—"

"Wait. You look freezing. Do you want a cup of tea or something?"

I shiver and hug my arms to my chest. "Are you sure?"

"Mint or apple spice?"

"Apple spice," I say, "if it's not a problem."

Annie opens her door a little. "Come on in."

I unlace my sneakers and leave them in the hallway before stepping into Annie's room. The first thing I see is one single bed. *How strange.* I always pictured Annie having a roommate.

As she fills an electric kettle with bottled water and plugs it into the wall, I settle onto her rug. It's a cozy room, with a fuzzy beanbag chair, a lava lamp, and photos of friends plastering the walls. I notice a half-packed suitcase by the closet and a banner running across her screen saver that says ONE MORE DAY TILL BREAK!

"Do you want honey in your tea?"

"Sure."

"That's how I like it, too."

Annie hands me a mug.

"Thanks."

"Virginia, right?" Annie says, settling onto the

 240

beanbag chair.

"Yeah."

"Virginia, it was brave of you to come up here, though I have to admit it weirded me out at first."

I attempt to sip my tea, but it's still too hot.

"How did you find my room?" Annie asks.

"The student directory in that glass building."

Annie is quiet as she blows the steam off her tea. "Can I say one thing about your ... about Byron?"

Annie pronounces *about* the Canadian way: *a-boot*.

I shrug. "Sure."

"What you said at the door, about him wrecking my life..."

"Yeah?"

"He hasn't."

"Really?"

Annie shakes her head and her hair spills over her chest, like a shawl. "What Byron did was awful. That's why I reported him to the campus authorities. I don't want him to think he can ever do that to another woman." Annie pauses and looks around her room. I can tell this is hard for her to talk about. "But as much as this has been a horrendous experience, my life isn't wrecked. I won't let him have that kind of power over me."

"What do you mean?"

"I had no control over what Byron did that night," Annie says. "But what happened the next morning, what will happen every morning for the rest of my life, that's up to me. I think people can choose to be victims or they can choose to be empowered and to carry on. That's what I want. To be empowered."

I stare at Annie. I'm completely speechless. I can't believe how much I identify with what she said—just with how things are in my family, how I've always let myself get treated.

"May I play a song for you?" Annie asks. "It's an early one by Ani DiFranco."

I nod.

Annie crawls across her floor. She slides a CD into her stereo and clicks until she reaches the right track.

"It's called 'Gratitude,'" she says. "It's really helped me get through this semester."

It turns out to be a song about a guy who invites a girl to sleep in his bed, promising it'll just be platonic, and then starts pressuring her to fool around. You can tell that Ani is angry, but at the same time she's also funny and strong and sassy.

By the time the song is over, I've got goose bumps on my arms.

"You remind me of my older sister," I say. "You'd like her a lot."

Annie smiles. "I bet I would. Because I already like her sister."

It takes me a few seconds to realize that she's talking about me.

242

*　　*　　*

As soon as I get home, I write a letter to Anaïs. I tell her about Byron, my crash diet, my burnt finger, Seattle, my broken toe, Annie Mills. I write and write until I've filled nine sheets of pale pink stationery. Then I fold the pages into an envelope and head into Mom's study to search for my sister's address.

Mom's desk is covered with papers and Post-its and books on adolescent psychology. After poking around for a few minutes, I locate her address book. I flip to the S's and there it is: Anaïs Shreves, care of the Peace Corps.

I always thought Mom was the gatekeeper to my sister, that I couldn't write her without Mom's permission. But Anaïs's address has been here all along. I just had to look.

CHAPTER TWENTY-SIX

The day before winter break has dragged more slowly than a snail on sleeping pills. I'm so exhausted that I've spent the entire day in a state of perpetual yawn. I stayed up until two in the morning studying for today's global studies exam. We had to regurgitate everything we learned all fall, complete with names, dates, and puncture wounds.

I set my alarm for five-thirty this morning so I could memorize the various nationalities in French for our test today, but I didn't rouse until ten to seven, so I skipped my shower, rushed to the bus, and bombed the quiz. The only nationality I could remember was *chinois*, which is Chinese.

In language arts we had to write an in-class essay about "Ostracism and Oppression," comparing and contrasting the various books we read this fall. In chemistry we were tested on

 244

stoichiometry, which I can barely pronounce, much less define.

I've decided that Brewster teachers definitely missed the lesson on holiday spirit.

Even Mr. Moony scheduled a test for today. I spent all of lunch memorizing circle theorems, but as I arrive in last period, Mr. Moony is sleeping at his desk. Behind him on the chalkboard, he's written:

Class—
I'm not feeling well this afternoon. The examination is rescheduled for after break.
Happy Holidays,
Clive Moony

A few kids fling their notebooks into the air. One guy erases "after break" and writes "never." Alyssa Wu suggests we send for Paul the School Nurse, but she's outvoted by the rest of the class, who point out that he might report it to the principal, who might replace Mr. Moony with a new geometry teacher who might actually make us work. As everyone rearranges their desks into clusters of three or four, I forge Mr. Moony's signature on a pass and take the back staircase down to Ms. Crowley's office.

I didn't see her during lunch period because she had a holiday party with the other language arts teachers, so I want to make sure to give her the card I bought for her. It has a picture of eight Great Danes pulling Santa's sleigh across a rooftop. Ms. Crowley and her husband are total Great Dane freaks. I wrote a long note inside, thanking her for being there for me this fall.

Ms. Crowley explodes into laughter as she slides my card out of the envelope.

I smile. "I thought you'd like it."

As she reads my note, I fiddle with my eyebrow ring. I was in a gushy mood when I wrote it, so I hope I didn't go too far.

"Oh, Virginia," she says, patting my arm, "it's been such a pleasure having you up here so much."

"Thanks."

Ms. Crowley traces her finger along the spine of the card. "I hope I'm not out of line saying this…"

"Saying what?" I ask, my shoulders tensing up.

"I've enjoyed spending all of these lunch periods together, but I want to make sure you're not isolating yourself from your peers. There are lots of nice kids at Brewster, if only you reached out, gave them a—"

Adrenaline surges through my body, propelling me to my feet. "I thought I was welcome here."

"You were." Ms. Crowley makes an uncomfortable face. "You still are. I'm just saying this because I care about you."

"If you cared about me, you wouldn't say something like that!" I shout.

I storm out of Ms. Crowley's office and race down the stairs, two at a time. I'm almost at my locker when I smack into Paul the School Nurse.

"Are you OK?" he asks.

"Perfect!" I shout.

I'm about to add *lovely, fine, and great* when I notice that Paul is wringing his hands together and staring anxiously out the front doors of Brewster, which are propped open.

That's when I see the ambulance parked on the street.

"What's going on?"

"It's Clive Moony," Paul says. "A student in his last-period class called 911 from her cell phone because he complained of chest pain."

I suck in my breath. I was up there only fifteen or twenty minutes ago. It must have happened right after I left. I can't believe it. I wonder who called 911. I wonder who ran down and got Paul. I wonder what the other kids did.

"Do they think it's a heart attack?" I ask.

"No one knows for sure," Paul says.

Paul and I walk to the front stoop. The air is so bitterly cold that it's hard to breathe. We watch as two paramedics slide a stretcher into the back of the ambulance. There's an oxygen mask on Mr. Moony's face. One person crawls in after him. Then the other jumps in and slams the door shut.

247

Seconds later the ambulance is speeding down the street, lights flashing and siren wailing.

The final bell rings.

Winter break has begun.

Chapter Twenty-Seven

My parents' friends, Marcia and Brad Lowenstein, always have their holiday party on the Saturday before Christmas. She's Baptist and he's Jewish, so it usually lands on one of the days of Hanukkah. They're raising their twin boys in both faiths, so they adorn their Connecticut house with dreidels and menorahs, Santas and mangers, five-pointed stars and six-pointed stars. Everyone gets dressed up. The parents drink too much eggnog. The teenagers pretend they've drunk too much eggnog. I wind up in the kiddie room with the preschool crew, watching *The Lion King* and wishing I could get run over by a reindeer.

And it's all happening tonight.

I still don't have a dress. Ever since the Saks incident, Mom hasn't mentioned my holiday outfit.

But I've decided I want something new to wear, so I wait until Mom has left for her step-aerobics class to ask Dad if I can borrow his credit card.

I take the subway down to Strawberry, where I try on about thirty dresses before finding the perfect one. It's purple stretch velvet, low cut, snug around my chest and loose in the tummy-hip-thigh region. The saleswoman tells me that if I pass it up, I'll regret it forever. I study my reflection in the mirror. I've never worn anything this risqué, but it strikes me that my breasts actually look vaguely sexy when they're not lost beneath layers of baggy clothing. I decide to go for it.

As soon as I get home, I slip on the new dress and peek into my parents' room. Mom is unpacking her gym bag.

"What do you think?" I ask, spinning around her room. The skirt billows out like an upside-down tulip.

"Very nice," Mom says.

"Thanks."

"It's not your usual style, is it?"

Actually, Mom, I want to say, *it's not YOUR usual style.*

"That's what I like about it," I say.

"Where did you get it?"

"Strawberry."

Mom places her sneakers in the rack hanging over her closet door. "Do you really think you

 250

should have gotten purple?"

I stop spinning. "Why not?"

"Purple doesn't go with your hair. Blonds should wear yellow or beige, something that isn't so domineering."

Fifteen minutes later, Mom leaves for a hair appointment. That's when I decide to have a little hair appointment of my own. I zip up my jacket and walk down to Ricky's, this wacky store that specializes in leopard-print undies and glittery makeup. The sales guy recommends a brand of hair dye called Special Effects. He explains that it lasts for three to six weeks, possibly longer with light hair. I select the shade "Pimpin' Purple."

As soon as I get home, I dig some rubber gloves out of the supply closet and lock myself in the bathroom. I turn on the shower, strip down, shampoo my hair, and follow the instructions on the Special Effects bottle. Forty minutes later, I emerge from the bathroom. My hair resembles a wad of grape-flavored Bubble Yum.

"Oh my god!" Mom gasps upon entering the apartment a few hours later.

I'm in the kitchen making a cup of hot chocolate. I'm wearing one of Anaïs's old Dartmouth sweatshirts and my flannel pajama bottoms.

"What have you done?" Mom clutches her collarbone. She appears to be asphyxiating.

"You said my hair didn't go with my dress," I say, matter-of-factly.

"Please tell me it's not permanent. That's all I want to hear."

"It's not permanent." I pour boiling water into my mug and watch the mini marshmallows bob to the surface.

"Really?"

"No. You just asked me to say that."

Tendons are straining out of Mom's neck like taut violin strings. "How long will it last?"

"Three to six weeks, possibly longer."

"Well," Mom says after a long silence, "at least you didn't dye it green."

Special Effects had a particularly offensive shade called "Iguana Green." I kick myself for not going that route.

Everyone at the Lowensteins' party gushes over my hair. With that and my cleavagey dress and my eyebrow ring, I make an impressive entrance. Dad escorts me around the room, commenting that the purple hair comes from *his* side of the family.

While we're in the buffet line, Byron makes a sniping remark about how I look like one of those Teletubby characters. He emphasizes the word "tubby." Before I can stop myself, I kick him in the shin really hard. I can tell it hurts because he looks like he wants to smack me. He slams down his plate of latkes and stomps away. I help myself to one of his potato pancakes.

Near the end of the evening, I'm trapped in a corner with Nan the Neurotic Nutritionist. She's spent the past ten minutes warbling on about organic produce and the chemicals they put into prepackaged foods.

"Speaking of chemicals," Nan says, gesturing to my purple head, "how did you decide to take the plunge?"

I glance at Mom. She's standing a few feet from me, sipping spiked punch and talking to a small, bespectacled woman. I can hear her explaining how Byron took time off from Columbia to re-evaluate his life, how it's hard always being an overachiever.

"I'm taking time off to reevaluate my hair color," I say. "It's hard always being a blond."

We're in the car on the way home from the Lowen-steins'. Dad is driving. Byron is up front keeping him company. Mom drank too much punch, so she's resting in the back with me. I'm staring out my foggy window, checking out Christmas decorations in people's yards.

"Ginny?" Mom says.

I turn toward her. Mom hasn't called me Ginny since I was five or six. "Yeah?"

"Remember what you said when we were shopping, about how you're not like me when I was younger?"

I nod as I think about that scene in Saks. My toe is nearly healed, so I'd rather not dwell on it anymore.

"I wish I'd had the nerve to dye my hair purple when I was your age."

I can't believe I'm hearing this. "You like my hair?"

"I'm not saying *that* much." Mom smiles sheepishly. The punch definitely has loosened her up. "But I do admire your chutzpah."

I stare at Mom. She stares back at me. We sit there for a second, staring and smiling at each other.

"Did Mom just use the word 'chutzpah'?" Byron laughs hoarsely. "Ms. Ozark, Arkansas, goes to a Hanukkah party and suddenly she's speaking Yiddish."

Mom looks out her window.

I look out mine.

"I like the word 'chutzpah'," Dad says. "It means courage and strength, but it sums it up in a way that only Yiddish can do."

"But *Mom* speaking Yiddish? She's so white bread."

I wipe the condensation from my window just in time to spot a huge plastic Santa propped on a rooftop, his tomato-red cheeks blinking in the night.

Yes, Mom.

Speaking Yiddish.

About me.

CHAPTER TWENTY-EIGHT

Christmas has never been very deck-the-hallsy around the Shreves household, and this year is no exception. I give Mom a gift certificate to Banana Republic. I give Dad a gift certificate to Sports Authority. I give Byron a gift certificate to Tower Records. He gives me the same gift certificate for the same amount, so we both keep our own. I use my gift certificate to buy *Like I Said*, the Ani DiFranco album with the song on it that Annie Mills played for me.

My parents give me a digital camera. That's what I asked for. I've been mulling over the idea of building a personal Web page, so I thought a digital camera would come in handy. At the very least, I can e-mail Shannon shots of my purple hair. She's already sent me some goofy pictures of her sticking out her completely healed tongue.

The day after Christmas, Mom and Dad fly to the Caribbean, where they're spending a week at a tropical golf resort. As soon as they leave, Byron takes over the apartment, strewing towels on the bathroom floor, leaving the TV on all the time, clogging the kitchen sink with crusty dishes.

I relocate to Mrs. Myers' apartment on the ninth floor. She's visiting her grandnephew in Florida, so I'm feeding her Siamese cats. I don't sleep in her bed, but I spend all my waking hours down there reading magazines, baking brownies, and watching reruns. The only times I go up to our apartment are to sleep or shower or e-mail Shannon, since Mrs. Myers doesn't have a computer.

I haven't spoken with anyone from school, so I don't know what happened with Mr. Moony. I don't know if he had a heart attack or if he's in the hospital or what. I still can't believe I saw him a few minutes before he was rushed off in an ambulance.

I considered calling Ms. Crowley to see what she knows, but then I remembered that she's spending the break with her in-laws in Vermont. I feel awful that I stormed out of her office last week. I know she only wanted to help me, but I guess it struck a raw nerve. As they say, the truth is always the hardest thing to hear.

*　　*　　*

257

It's New Year's Eve afternoon.

I've just arrived at the kickboxing class that Dr. Love recommended. For my New Year's resolution, I'm vowing to do something good for my body and soul. A daily hot fudge sundae almost won out, if it weren't for the body aspect. Then I considered another crash diet, but that seems to trash my soul.

It's a small class, only nine other girls. They're all around my age. The teacher's name is Tisha. She's got cornrowed hair, a full figure, and an orange spandex outfit. She looks like she could kick some serious ass.

Tisha has us jump rope and do jumping jacks to warm up. After we stretch, she hands out gloves and this long, black cloth material. She shows newcomers how to wrap the material around our hands, to protect them. It's supposed to go around each finger, our knuckles, and our wrists, but it's so confusing that one girl jokes by binding her hand to her foot, which makes us all crack up.

We spend the rest of the hour learning how to punch and kick various bags. At one point, as we're punching what she calls the "heavy bags," Tisha tells us to visualize someone who pisses us off and let them have it. I think about Byron and end up punching so hard that Tisha has the other girls pause to admire my efforts.

After class I'm drenched in sweat, but I feel

energized. It's strange how taking all that anger out on the punching bag actually makes me feel better than I have in a long time.

"I'm thrilled to have you join us," Tisha says to me as I pull my sweatpants on over my shorts. "I can tell you have a lot of potential."

"Thanks," I say.

Tisha and I discuss the schedule and fees and then I head to the subway with two other girls from the class. They introduce themselves as Sammie and Phoebe. Phoebe is really small and chatty. She says she started this class a few months ago, after her parents insisted she take up an athletic activity. Sammie is much quieter, but she smiles at me a few times and I can tell she's nice, just more on the shy side.

We all chat for a few stops on the subway. They both rave about my purple hair. Phoebe gets off at Ninety-sixth Street and asks Sammie to call her as soon as she gets home. Sammie and I ride down to Seventy-ninth Street together. She tells me how her dad is in town for the holidays, so she's showing him around the city.

When we get to my stop, I wave goodbye.

"See you at the next class," she says.

"Yeah," I say. "Happy New Year!"

Shannon and I have promised to call each other tonight, have a bicoastal drink, ring in the New Year.

I call Shannon around ten. Liam and Nina have just left for the evening, so our first order of business is intoxication. I carry the cordless phone into the kitchen because Dad keeps the vodka in the freezer. I squeeze the phone between my ear and shoulder, pour some vodka into a glass, and fill the rest with orange juice.

"I'm taking some white wine," Shannon says, giggling, "and mixing it with cherry Kool-Aid."

"Shannon Iris," I say, "you are such a boozer."

Neither of us has ever raided our parents' alcohol supply before, so we're totally buzzed just from the excitement of it. I carry my drink into my bedroom. Shannon and I chat for about an hour and then we decide to take a quick bathroom break.

"I'll call you back in five minutes," Shannon says. "That way we can split the phone bill."

"Make sure to fill up your wineglass!"

"Who's the boozer now?"

I teeter a little when I stand up. After peeing, I head into the kitchen and pour another shot of vodka. This time I mix it with cranberry juice.

"Go easy on Dad's vodka," Byron calls from the living room. "It's not cheap stuff."

Byron is slumped on the couch, watching the Times Square ball drop on TV. He's been grumpy all day because no one invited him out tonight.

"Whatever," I say. I pour some additional vodka into my glass.

The phone rings, so I spring for it.

"Shan?"

"Drunk yet?"

"Getting there," I say.

"Me, too!"

Shannon and I giggle and tell stupid jokes until the clocks hit midnight in New York. Then we shriek and scream and jump on our beds. We're both a little sloshed. And it doesn't help that we've been pretending to slur our words for the past twenty minutes.

"Happy New Year, shhhwweeetheart," Shannon garbles.

"Shhhame to you, Shannon Ireeeeesh."

After we hang up, I make my way into the kitchen to get some water. I'm so wobbly that I have to clutch the walls. My cheeks feel flushed and I'm smiling for no reason in particular.

"Feeling OK?" Byron asks, clutching a fork and staring into the open fridge.

I scowl. "Why should you care?"

I attempt to pour a glass of water, but half of it splashes onto the counter. Ever since our argument a few weeks ago, there's been some serious tension between Byron and me. In the past I would have been the one to back down, but now I'm more than happy to keep my pistols drawn.

"It's just that your first time drinking can be the worst," Byron says.

"How do you know it's my first time?"

"I'm just remembering back from when I was in high school."

"And what does *that* have to do with me?"

Byron shrugs as he takes a container of potato salad out of the fridge. "It's crazy thinking about high school, Gin. I thought I had my whole life set, but then one wrong turn and look at me now."

I hold onto the dishwasher to steady myself. "Do you regret what you did to Annie Mills?"

Byron stabs a potato chunk with his fork. "Of course I do."

"Well, you definitely let me down," I say. Normally, I wouldn't be this honest with Byron, but the vodka is doing strange things to my brain.

"What do you mean?"

I stare at my brother. In the past several months, I've been so upset because he hurt Annie Mills. But it hits me that I'm angry on my own behalf, too. Partially because of the date rape, but mostly for how Byron has acted toward me over the past several years.

"I used to worship you," I say, "even though you didn't treat me with the same respect that I treated you."

"You can't put people on pedestals." Byron snaps the lid back on the container. "They'll just disappoint you."

"You let me put you up there, so you've got to

 262

take some responsibility."

Byron leans against the counter. He doesn't respond, but I know that he heard me.

I head into my bedroom and collapse on my bed. The walls start spinning around me. I feel like I'm in that twister scene from *The Wizard of Oz*, but instead of farmhouses and witches on bicycles whizzing through the air, it's ideas.

I'm thinking about Ms. Crowley's comment about how I isolate myself from my peers. I'm thinking about my new digital camera. I'm thinking about how much I've enjoyed trying new things, like my eyebrow ring and my purple hair. I'm thinking about those girls from kickboxing and how easy it was to meet new people, much easier than I always thought it would be.

All of a sudden, I feel nauseous. I stumble into the bathroom, open the toilet lid, and puke.

Happy New Year, I think to myself as I swish a mouthful of water and spit it into the sink.

CHAPTER TWENTY-NINE

I'm actually excited about starting school again. Today is our first day back, so I'm wearing the polyester orange shirt that I bought at that vintage shop in Seattle. I wore it once over break and I like the way it looks.

I factor in some extra time to do my hair. It's faded a little, so I want to jazz it up for school. I experiment with a few styles before settling on two antenna-like pigtails sprouting from either side. I rub purple glitter around my eyes to add to the cosmic effect.

I'm on my way to my locker when I pass Alyssa Wu. She's wearing a cream-colored sweater and a matching cap. I bet she knitted them herself. They look great with her shiny black hair.

"Cool hair!" she says.

"Thanks."

Alyssa walks to my locker with me. As I turn my combination, I ask, "How was your break?"

"Fine. Boring. Same as usual," she says. "What about you?"

The principal's voice comes over the PA system. She summons us to the auditorium for an assembly before first period.

I slam my locker shut. "Do you know what that's about?"

Alyssa shrugs. "Not a clue."

As Alyssa and I settle into some aisle seats, I notice that Brinna Livingston is sitting in Brie's usual Queen Bee spot. To her right is Briar Schwartz, Lady in Waiting #1. To her left is a skinny sophomore named Brittany Felsen.

I glance around for Brie, only to see her sitting a few rows back. She looks awful—pale and small, like a flutter of wind could blow her away. I wonder if she's been bumped from her position of power, if Brinna now holds the throne, if Brittany Felsen is the replacement Bri-girl.

The principal walks onto the stage and taps the microphone a few times.

"Welcome back, students and faculty," she says. "I'm sorry to start the new year with tragic news, but as most of you know, Clive Moony had some heart trouble the day before break." The principal daubs her eyes with a tissue. "It turned out to be a major heart attack that took a toll on his body. Mr. Moony passed away on New Year's Day."

The auditorium is completely silent. I glance at Alyssa, but her face is sinking into her hands. My eyes and nose sting like I want to cry, but the tears won't come. The principal launches into a speech about how Mr. Moony taught math for forty-one years, directed the school choir for thirty years, won Model Brewster Teacher seven times. When she tells us that condolence cards can be sent to his widow, I'm shocked by the realization that Mr. Moony had a life outside of the Pythagorean theorem.

"In honor of Clive Moony," the principal says, "I'd like to have a moment of silence."

As we sit in silence, I can't help but feel like something is wrong. I mean, Mr. Moony was *never* quiet, what with his never-ending parade of songs with our names in them.

Suddenly, a guy near the back belts out, *"Mr. Moon, Moon, bright and shiny moon, oh won't you please shine down on me?"*

A few kids crane their necks to stare at him, but most people join in the song.

"Mr. Moon, Moon, bright and shiny moon, oh won't you please shine down on me?"

Those who don't know the lyrics hum or sway from side to side. I sing, even though tears are trickling down my face. Most people in the auditorium are at least sniffling, if not all-out crying. I have a feeling we're all thinking the same thing. We hated the way Mr. Moony serenaded us, but we're going to miss it now that he's gone.

As I'm filing out of the auditorium, I pass a teary-eyed Ms. Crowley.

"Virginia." She wraps her arms around me.

"I'm so sorry for how I acted before break," I say. "I don't know what—"

Ms. Crowley cuts me off. "No, *I'm* sorry. I completely overstepped my boundaries. I've been feeling horrible ever since I said it."

"I'm glad you did. I needed to hear that, especially from someone I respect."

Ms. Crowley squeezes my shoulder. "What have you got first period?"

"Global studies. Why?"

"I've got something for you. I was going to give it to you before break. Can you come up to my office? I'll write you a late pass."

On our way upstairs, I tell Ms. Crowley about my new idea. I've decided that rather than just building my own homepage, I want to start an online webzine where kids can rant about anything on their minds. I want to make it an official Brewster club, so I'll need a teacher to sponsor the idea.

"I'd be happy to," Ms. Crowley says as she hands me a wrapped present. "Just bring me the forms and I'll sign away."

I rip open the paper. Ms. Crowley has given me a book called *Body Outlaws*. There are several pictures of women on the cover—all shapes and sizes and races—flexing their biceps, chowing down, flaunting tattoos.

"It's a fantastic book," Ms. Crowley says. "All essays by young women who are rebelling against body norms."

I thumb through the index. There's a chapter called "The Butt" and another called "Fishnets, Feather Boas, and Fat."

"Make sure to read the inscription," Ms. Crowley adds.

I flip to the inside flap, where she's written:

"I thought at last that it was time to roll up the crumpled skin of the day, with its arguments and its impressions and its anger and its laughter, and cast it into the hedge."
—Virginia Woolf, "A Room of One's Own"

I've never really *gotten* Virginia Woolf before, but this passage seems to makes sense. It's about throwing out old notions and re-evaluating what you've always thought. At least I think so. I guess it makes more sense on an emotional level than on an intellectual one.

Maybe that's the way it's supposed to be.

As soon as I've read *Body Outlaws*, I think I'll give my namesake another chance.

CHAPTER THIRTY

I can't believe how much has changed in the first week back at school. I don't know whether it's Mr. Moony's death or just my perception of things, but the climate at Brewster feels much warmer. Popular kids are waving at regular kids in the halls. Regular kids are helping dorky kids gather papers if they drop a notebook down the stairs. Dorky kids aren't smirking behind their hands when a popular kid screws up in class.

When I pointed this out to Alyssa Wu, she summed it up as "the Postdeath Touchy-Feely Period."

"It's like how my whole family got along for a few weeks after my uncle died," she said one morning as we were waiting for global studies to begin. "Don't be fooled by it, though."

"But isn't it a good thing?"

"Rule number one of the Postdeath Touchy-Feely Period: Enjoy it while it lasts," Alyssa said. "Rule number two of the Postdeath Touchy-Feely Period: It doesn't last."

I had to laugh. It was surprising to hear that someone else in this world thinks the way I do, in terms of lists and rules. I haven't written a list in forever, not since everything happened with Byron. But I'm starting to feel ideas come into my head again.

"I still can't believe I was in his class a few minutes before the heart attack," I said.

"I know," Alyssa said. "It was so scary. I kept thinking that I shouldn't have listened to everyone. I should have gotten the school nurse at the beginning of the period."

"There's no way you could have known."

"But still."

I've been eating lunch with Alyssa and a few other girls every day, even though Ms. Crowley keeps reminding me that I'm welcome in her office. I'm really starting to like Alyssa. She comes across as a little weird at first, but she's actually pretty cool. She fidgets constantly—her fingers, wrists, ankles—every joint is always in motion. That's why she knits. She says she needs to be doing something with her hands, otherwise she'd drive herself and everyone in her vicinity crazy.

Alyssa is a pop-music junkie. She goes to Times

Square almost every day after school to join the crowds cheering up at the MTV studios during *Total Request Live*. She invited me to join her yesterday afternoon. As we jumped and hooted and froze our butts off, I learned another thing about Alyssa. She can scream louder than anyone I know.

That's why I've asked her to get everyone's attention today.

It's lunchtime. I'm about to make an announcement about my new webzine. Over the past week, I've filled out all the necessary paperwork to make it an official school club. I've even received a modest budget, enough to buy a domain name and get it hosted on the Web. The only things I need now are writers, editors, and people who can do graphic design.

Alyssa stands on a chair and cups her hands around her mouth to create the megaphone effect.

"Romans, cafeteria-men!" she bellows.

People pause midbite and glance curiously up at her.

She continues, "Virginia Shreves has an important announcement, so lend her an ear."

I take a sip of Diet Pepsi, swish the taco shell out of my braces, and climb on a chair next to Alyssa. I tell everyone that I'm creating a webzine where people can bitch, rant, and rave about whatever is on their minds.

"The first meeting is in the computer cluster

272

after school today," I say.

Alyssa chimes in that it'll look good on college applications, something that would inspire most Brewsterites to dance on scorching embers.

A few people visit our table to say they'll swing by the meeting. One girl tells me she can't make it, but jots her e-mail address on a napkin so I can let her know about future gatherings.

I'm tossing my tray into the trash when I spot Froggy. He's heading out of the cafeteria with some friends. We've spoken a little since school started again. He complimented my purple hair in the hallway. I borrowed his whiteout in French. That's about the extent of it. I *did* see him lugging his trombone up the front steps of school, so that ruled out my sold-horn-for-laser-surgery theory.

"Hey, Froggy," I call out. "Wait up!"

Froggy glances over his shoulder. I can hear him telling his friends to go on ahead.

"What's up?" Froggy asks. He looks pretty surprised.

I feel my cheeks turning pink. "I was just wondering if you were coming to my meeting today."

Froggy tweaks his nose a few times. "I hadn't thought about it."

"I could really use your Web design skills."

Froggy doesn't respond.

"More than that," I add, "it would be nice to hang out again."

273

Before I can say anything I'll later regret, I turn and start toward my table.

"Virginia?" Froggy calls after me.

I spin around. "Yeah?"

"I'll be there."

I race to the computer cluster after last period. Krishna said we can hold our meetings there. He's even offered to assist with the techie aspects of getting a website up and running.

I'm so excited about the turnout—eight kids, including me and Alyssa—that I won't let myself feel bad that Froggy is a no-show. I glance at Alyssa, who gives me a sympathetic smile. I filled her in on the brief history of Froggy, so she had her fingers and toes crossed that he'd be at the meeting.

"One more minute," Alyssa mouths, gesturing to her watch.

We wait for two and a half minutes. Finally, I sit on top of a desk, cross one knee over the other, and turn my notebook to a fresh page. I'm just introducing myself when Froggy walks in, his hands jammed in his pockets. I wave at Froggy, take a deep breath, and suggest we go around the room and say our names.

After everyone's introduced themselves, I talk a little about my vision for the webzine. I make sure to add that it will reflect what's going on in *all* of our heads. Basically, I want us to voice the things that people don't ordinarily talk about.

Then I bring up the first order of business—deciding what to call the webzine. Froggy rolls his chair over to a computer station and volunteers to check which domain names are available.

"How about *Rant*?" suggests one ninth-grader.

Froggy types it into the computer. "Taken," he says after a moment.

A girl named Nikki asks, "What about *Dirty Laundry*, since that's what we're going to air?"

"Good idea," one kid says.

Froggy is quiet for a second. "Also taken."

This goofy junior named Hudson says, "We should call it *MBS*, like Model Brewster Student, except it would really stand for *Major Bullshit*."

"I wish," I say, laughing, "but they'd probably cut our school funding."

Alyssa is propped on the back of a chair, knitting something long and violet. "Do you have any ideas, Virginia?"

I'm quiet for a second. "What about something like *Earthquake*, because we want to shake things up?"

A few kids nod, but after Froggy types "earthquake" into the computer he says, "Taken by some science lab."

"What about *Earth*quack?" Alyssa asks. "We're shaking stuff up, but we're also going to expose

275

things for what they are and what they aren't."

We all crack up. Hudson makes a duck sound.

Froggy types "earthquack" and then turns in his chair so he's facing everyone. "Surprisingly," he says, grinning, "*Earthquack* is up for grabs."

Everyone applauds.

"Let's have a show of hands," I call out. "How many people want *Earthquack*?"

The vote is unanimous.

Earthquack is born.

CHAPTER THIRTY-ONE

Life has become a blur of school, *Earthquack*, and wailing with Alyssa in Times Square. Even my parents commented that I'm rarely home anymore, and I didn't think they noticed those kinds of things.

What shocked me more than anything is that I didn't turn on the TV for three straight days last week. I didn't even realize it until I went to watch *Entertainment Tonight* and couldn't find the remote control. By the time I finally retrieved it from under a couch cushion, I'd gotten a brainstorm for *Earthquack*, so I ran into my room to scribble some stuff in my notebook.

I've been putting so much energy into *Earthquack*. We agreed to convene once a week, but the core group of us has been sitting together at lunch every day, so it usually becomes an informal meeting.

We're shooting to launch *Earthquack* by the beginning of February. People have already shown me drafts of their ideas. Nikki is writing the uncensored story of Theo Brewster, with an emphasis on his alcoholic, rum-running days. Hudson is writing a humorous call-to-arms, urging the regular and dorky kids to infiltrate the popular courtyard armed with candy cigarettes. Alyssa is gathering lyrics to Mr. Moony's favorite songs because we're going to post a special tribute to him. She's also writing a scathing essay about how because she's Asian, the Brewster administration always calls on her when they're taking pictures for their promotional fliers.

When she told everyone that idea, Nikki laughed and said, "You tell 'em!" Nikki is black, so she's probably on the diversity roster as well. I was tempted to say something about how Brewster hasn't shown any interest in *weight* diversity, but I'm not quite ready to go there yet.

One day at lunch, Froggy brought along Sarah, that ninth-grader with the ski-jump nose. I wanted to drown myself in an industrial-sized vat of chocolate pudding, but then I heard her tell Hudson that Froggy's parents and her parents are old friends, so she and Froggy are practically siblings. It also turns out that Sarah is a grammar whiz, so she's going to be our copyeditor.

Froggy has put together some hilarious ideas for

the design. My favorite is an image of a yellow duck taking a bite out of our planet. When it does, several ducklings jump out of the earth's core and waddle across the screen, quacking wildly. He printed out what he called a "screen shot"—basically just a copy of the page—for me, and I taped it up inside my locker.

I have to admit I still have feelings for Froggy. But since I can't imagine he'd ever want to go public with me, I'll have to settle for just being friends. My hormones are telling me to obey the Fat Girl Code of Conduct and invite Froggy to fool around with me in private again. Then I remember how hiding our relationship made me feel lousy. Even so, whenever I catch Froggy looking my way in French class, I feel a thrum-thrumming between my legs.

Speaking of French, I'm considering dropping it after this year. It's actually not that bad anymore because Mademoiselle Kiefer has undergone a 180-degree transformation. It all started when our new geometry teacher—the one who replaced Mr. Moony—delivered a dozen white roses to the language office. They were addressed to *Joanne Kiefer, a natural woman*. Mademoiselle Kiefer must have had a whopping case of sexual frustration because she's now as sunny as Saint-Tropez. She's even talking about doing a special unit on Valentine's Day vocabulary. But I've finally come to terms

279

with the fact that, regardless of my Shreves lineage, I'm simply not meant to *parler français*.

I arranged a special meeting with the Chinese teacher. He said that if I take an intensive course over the summer, I can join the sophomores in September and thus complete my three-year language requirement by graduation. Alyssa's parents are from Beijing, so she's offered to tutor me. She's already taught me how to say *hello*, *thank you*, and *fuck off* in Mandarin.

I've gone to four more kickboxing classes. I love it, even though I'm so sore some days I can hardly sneeze. But it feels incredible to kick and sweat for a solid hour, to channel my aggression into a punching bag. I'm starting to feel stronger, to see my stomach and arms tightening up.

Dad must have noticed the difference. Last Sunday we went to a Knicks game together. I was surprised when he invited me because that's something he always does with Byron. But Dad and I have been communicating a little more recently, ever since he drove me to the airport that morning. A few weeks ago, I worked up the nerve to tell him I felt bad he didn't bring me to that Yankees playoff game last fall, so maybe the Knicks tickets were his way of making it up to me.

We were at Madison Square Garden. I'd been cheering and springing up and down and lusting after a certain sexy brown-eyed forward. As I settled back into my seat, Dad turned to me.

"You know, Ginny," he said, "you really look like you're slimming down."

A few months ago, that kind of compliment would have made my day. But I don't want that kind of feedback from my parents anymore. I don't want them to think they can discuss my body like it's the weather forecast on 1010 WINS.

"Dad? We're trying to be more open with each other, right?"

Dad nodded, but his forehead was wrinkled in confusion.

"Then I have to tell you that I'd rather you don't talk about my body. It's just not yours to discuss."

Dad looked like he swallowed a basketball. "I'm sorry," he said. "I hadn't realized…"

"It's OK. Now you know."

I've been thinking a lot lately about why I overeat. I've decided that food is my ultimate comfort. If I'm lonely or depressed, a bowl of pasta or a plate of cookies will cheer me up. I know I have to learn healthier ways to deal with it, but it can't happen overnight. And I can't do it for anyone but myself.

That's why I haven't told Mom I'm taking kickboxing. I'm paying for it out of my own money and everything. I just don't want this to become something I'm doing to please her, to make her proud of me.

I *did* tell Teri the Tiny Gym Teacher. She gave me a form and said that if I have Tisha sign it after every kickboxing class, I can place out of gym.

Thanks to kickboxing, I've been able to go to the computer cluster during gym periods. My grades slipped a little last fall, so I'm determined to bring them up again. Especially since I've decided I probably don't want to go to college in the Arctic Circle. I think I'd like to apply to an artsy school with a good writing program, like Vassar or Wesleyan.

That's what my language arts teacher was talking about the other day. I'm really loving language arts now. We started a new unit a few weeks ago called "Women and Power," so we're reading this amazing book called *The Red Tent*, which is about biblical stories retold from the perspective of women.

Only when I'm completely done with my homework do I let myself work on *Earthquack*. I'm writing a list for the webzine, my first one in months. It's also the first list ever that I'm going to show people. No, not just *people*. Many, many people. The entire Web-surfing universe. I still can't believe I'm going to take the plunge. It makes me jittery just thinking about it. But I'm tired of always hiding what's going on and acting like things are OK even when they aren't.

Here's what I've written so far:

The Earth, My Butt, and Other Big, Round Things
by Virginia Shreves

1. My best friend moved to the other side of the earth for the entire school year. I thought I couldn't survive without her. While I still miss her like crazy, I think it's good that I've had to venture out on my own.

2. Besides, if she hadn't gone to Walla Walla (home of the big, round onion!), I wouldn't have been able to run away to Seattle for Thanksgiving and get an eyebrow ring and escape my stress-filled home (see #4).

3. I've never been a fan of my butt. Too big, too round, blah, blah, blah. But when grooving outside the MTV studios in Times Square, it's much more fun to shake your booty when you actually HAVE a booty to shake, not just a bony excuse for a rear end.

4. OK, so not all big, round things are great. Definitely not the meteor-sized lump I got in my throat last October when I found out my brother was being suspended from college for doing something horrible. But it gave me an important reality check about him, about my family, about myself.

5. Speaking of last fall, this isn't round, but it's definitely big. It's an apology. Last fall I was really mean to someone special. I hope you know who

you are (hint: Mondays after school). I wish I could say I was temporarily possessed by an evil alien, but the truth is just that I was going through a hard time.

6. Another big, round, not-so-pleasant thing: a head of lettuce. I'm going to state it—here, now, and forever. I hate lettuce. I've always hated lettuce. So maybe my mom is a skinny, lettuce-eating fiend, but I don't have to be, too. There are ways to eat healthy that don't involve rabbit cuisine.

7. And finally, let's face it. If you had a small, puny present and a big, round present, which one would you open first? The big, round one, right? Who ever said smaller is better? NO ONE, that's who!

CHAPTER THIRTY-TWO

It's an unseasonably warm Saturday afternoon. One of those days when the air is mild, icicles are dripping outside my window, and I want to throw all my winter clothes down the garbage chute. Of course, there will probably be a blizzard tomorrow, but on a day like this, it feels like the balmy weather will last forever.

I'm crouched in front of my mirror, trying on the tiny gold eyebrow ring that Mom brought me from the Caribbean. When I first opened the velvet box, I thought she was giving me a pair of earrings, but then I realized there was only one ring inside.

"Is this an…" I was so shocked I couldn't finish my sentence.

"If you're going to have facial jewelry, you shouldn't wear silver, not with your complexion."

"That's my Phyl," Dad said, tickling her waist.

"If you can't beat 'em, at least make sure they have the right metal."

Mom swatted him playfully and I cracked up. I'm realizing that sometimes it's easier to laugh off annoying Mom-isms than get angry at them. Besides, it's a cute eyebrow ring, much nicer than anything I could afford.

Byron is moving back to Columbia today. He's not going to the dorms, though. He'll be living in an off-campus basement apartment with a few grad students. It was Byron's choice, but he made it with strong pressure from Dean Briggs. It sounds like the rugby team will take him back, but he's been kicked off debate and has to undergo mandatory counseling for the entire semester.

Byron seems to be taking it all pretty hard—the off-campus stuff and the counseling and the debate team. It doesn't help that Mom and Dad are cross-country skiing in Connecticut this weekend, so Byron has to move all by himself. And there's no big brunch today, like my parents have had at the beginning of every other semester.

I could tell Byron felt bad when he woke up this morning. He kept making comments like, "They're gone?" and "They didn't even leave a note?" and "They just left without saying goodbye?"

I was tempted to say, *Join the club. That's how they've treated me for fifteen years.* But instead I toasted us both a bagel and made two mugs of

 286

hot chocolate.

Ever since New Year's Eve, Byron's been nicer to me than he's been in years. I still haven't forgiven him for what he did to Annie Mills, but he's the only brother I have, so I can't hate him forever. I don't think we'll ever be as close as when we were kids, but maybe that's OK.

I hear Byron heaving as he carries crates to the service elevator.

"Byron?" I call from my bedroom.

"Yeah?"

"Can you come here for a second?"

Byron approaches my doorway. He's wearing faded jeans and a sweat-soaked shirt. "What's up?"

"How would you like a full-length mirror for your new room?"

"You don't want your mirror?"

"I *never* wanted my mirror."

"I'll take it," Byron says. "But let me know if you ever want it back."

Byron and I lift the mirror together. Once we've loaded it into the elevator, I help him haul the rest of his stuff out of the apartment and into the rental truck.

After Byron drives off, I walk into the lobby of our building and check the mail. I'm thumbing through a stack of bills for my parents when I come across a handwritten envelope from Anaïs, addressed to me. I step into the elevator.

Dear Ginny,

Thanks for your letter! I'm so sorry about everything that's been happening. It reminded me of why I had to escape to Africa. I was suffocated by Mom's denial, by our family's pressure to fit a perfect mold at all costs. I'm sure you know what I'm talking about.

I promise a longer letter very soon, but I just wanted to say that in spite of everything, you sound better than ever.

Love,

Anaïs

When I get upstairs, I put the letter back in its envelope. It's strange to see Anaïs writing about the whole perfect-family thing. I'm starting to wonder if that's changing, if Byron's date rape shook everything up.

The phone rings. I make a dive for it.

"Hello?"

It's Mom, calling from her cell phone. "We're driving home from Connecticut."

"But it's only Saturday afternoon."

"The snow is too slushy for skiing," Mom says.

Dad says something in the background.

"Oh, yes," Mom adds. "We've gotten last-minute tickets to an exclusive film screening this evening. Would you like to come along?"

"Thanks, but I can't."

288

"Why not?"

"I'm getting together with some friends for dinner."

"Can't you get out of it?" Mom asks. "This is a once-in-a-lifetime opportunity."

"Nope," I say. "Sorry."

Mom laughs. "You really are a Shreves."

"What do you mean?"

"You do exactly what you want." Mom pauses before adding, "If I don't see you before you leave, have fun tonight."

"Thanks."

As I'm hanging up, I think about how I've always felt very *un*-Shreves, like I belonged in a clan of plump, blond underachievers. Now that I've been deemed an official family member, I'm not even sure I *want* that affiliation. Does "doing exactly what I want" mean not thinking about other people's feelings? Because that's just not the kind of person I am.

Maybe it can mean whatever I want it to mean, like taking care of myself and not letting people walk all over me.

Yes, that's much more like it.

I wear jeans, a long undershirt, and my WALLA WALLA IS FOR LOVERS sweatshirt. I excavated it from under my bed last night and threw it in the wash. I'm also wearing the violet scarf that Alyssa

289

knitted for me. It's so long I can wrap it around my neck three times.

I grab my digital camera and head over to Central Park. I'm meeting up with the Earthquackers at Belvedere Castle. We're going to Pizzeria Uno for dinner, but first we're doing a photo shoot so we can post pictures of us on the premiere issue of *Earthquack*. Froggy thought the castle would establish our regal status.

Most of the others are already there when I arrive. Some are climbing the stairs to an upper turret. Others are throwing ice chunks into Turtle Pond. Alyssa is chatting with Hudson. I know she has a crush on him, so I leave her alone.

"Nice sweatshirt." Froggy bumps his hip against mine.

"Thanks," I say, bumping him back.

"Virginia?"

"Yeah?"

"Do you know what they say about a frog in a castle?"

"No ... what?"

Froggy gets a shy smile on his face and rubs his nose a few times. "If you kiss him, he'll turn into a prince."

I glance around at the other kids. According to the Fat Girl Code of Conduct, public displays of affection are a cardinal no-no.

"Right here?" I ask.

Froggy nods.

"Right now?"

He nods again.

So I lean forward, close my eyes, and kiss Froggy
Welsh the Fourth.

Right on the lips.

Right in front of everybody.

LOVE AND OTHER
FOUR-LETTER WORDS
Carolyn Mackler

Sammie Davis never expected sweet sixteen to be perfect. But then she didn't expect her parents to separate either, or to have to leave her cosy life in suburbia for a tiny apartment in New York City. She begins a hot and humid summer struggling with feelings of resentment, anger ... and lust for the Johnny Depp look-alike in her apartment block. As the vacation rolls on, she makes friends and breaks friends, finds new depths to the word *love*, and comes to understand that with it come other four-letter words. Like *hate*; *loss*; *gain*. But most important of all, *grow*.

"I love Carolyn Mackler and welcome her lively debut novel! *Love and Other Four-Letter Words* will grab the reader from the first page."
Judy Blume

"Carolyn Mackler is a wonderful new talent."
Paula Danziger

PLANET JANET
Dyan Sheldon

Friday 22 December
I don't want to end up shallow and superficial like
so many other people (e.g. my family). I'm going
to be intense, serious, and spend a lot of time nur-
turing my soul. I'm also going to dress mainly in
black.

Meet Janet. She's determined to explore Life's
True Essence, despite the countless hurdles in her
way (i.e. her mother the Mad Cow, a tragically lost
mobile, the trials of Romantic Love etc.). But while
she splashes around the Deep End of the Pool of
Life, could Janet be missing what's happening on
dry land?

READ MY LIPS
Jana Novotny Hunter

This Deaf City war has been going on too long! It's time signers and speakers learned to get along.

Cat's had enough of the in-fighting at her school. So what if some students, like her, use sign language and others use speech? With the end of school looming, they're going to need all the help they can get to cope with the scary, hearing world of "outside". Which is why Cat decides to learn to speak again, despite her best friend's opposition. And when she falls for a speaker, she risks losing everything.

But Cat is determined that her voice will be heard...

FISH FEET
Veronica Bennett

Erik Shaw loves dancing and wants to audition for the Royal Ballet School. But that means making some tough decisions – such as giving up the Falcons football team and letting down old friends. Then there's Ruth, a fellow ballet dancer to whom Erik is becoming increasingly attracted. Can their relationship survive the rigours of practice and competition? And has Erik got the strength of will as well as the talent to achieve his goal?

STONER & SPAZ
Ron Koertge

Ben Bancroft is the invisible man.

Nicknamed Spaz because of the cerebral palsy that he has had since birth, Ben's a real loner. Living with his overprotective grandmother, he escapes whenever he can to the decrepit Rialto Theatre to watch old movies – and it's here, one fateful Friday evening, that he runs into Colleen Minou. Drugged up, outspoken, clad in ripped tights and a neon miniskirt, she's the kind of trouble Ben's spent his life avoiding. But when Colleen climbs into the seat beside him and rests a woozy head on his shoulder, it's the start of a relationship that will alter Ben's life ... for ever.

THURSDAY'S CHILD
Sonya Hartnett

The creature held a great bundle of something tied up in a rag. For a moment we stared, not recognizing him, but who else could it have been, who else but wandering Tin.

We saw his naked limbs, his waxy skin, his discoloured hair, his hooking razor-sharp nails. He raised his lashy eyes to us and we saw a face on its way to another world. Da murmured, "Jesus."

During the long, hungry years of the Great Depression, Harper Flute watches with a child's clear eyes her family's struggle to survive on the hot and impoverished land. As life on the surface grows harsher, her little brother Tin – "born on a Thursday and so fated to his wanderings" – escapes ever deeper into a subterranean world of darkness and troubling secrets as lives are changed for ever.

Thursday's Child is a gripping new novel by a writer of startling originality.

"A complex and haunting tale that will mesmerise readers of all ages." *The Bookseller*

WINNER OF THE GUARDIAN CHILDREN'S
FICTION AWARD